"Man, your dog can run..."

Charlotte chuckled. "He loves it. I have a big fenced-in yard, and he races the cars on the street."

A crack echoed through the trees.

Dennis yanked his gun from his holster, grabbed Charlotte's arm and tugged her near a tree. He scanned the woods. Where had the gunshot come from?

"Theo, now!" The dog raced back and fell in beside Charlotte.

Another shot rang out, and a chunk of bark splintered mere inches from his temple. He pushed Charlotte's head down and grabbed his radio.

"Shots fired. Finding safety." A specific location wasn't an option on an open channel. He prayed his deputies knew him well enough to determine where he'd head.

Dennis itched to go after the shooter, but he had no choice but to get Charlotte and Theo out of danger.

He jerked on her sleeve and pulled her with him. "We have to get out of here."

Two-time Genesis Award winner **Sami A. Abrams** and her husband live in Northern California, but she'll always be a Kansas girl at heart. She enjoys visiting her two grown children and spoiling their sweet fur babies. Most evenings, if Sami's not watching sports, you'll find her engrossed in a romantic suspense novel. She thinks a crime plus a little romance is the recipe for a great story. Visit her at www.samiaabrams.com.

Books by Sami A. Abrams

Love Inspired Suspense

Deputies of Anderson County

Buried Cold Case Secrets
Twin Murder Mix-Up
Detecting Secrets

Visit the Author Profile page at LoveInspired.com.

DETECTING SECRETS

SAMI A. ABRAMS

LOVE INSPIRED SUSPENSE
INSPIRATIONAL ROMANCE

LOVE INSPIRED® SUSPENSE
INSPIRATIONAL ROMANCE

ISBN-13: 978-1-335-58830-2

Detecting Secrets

Love Inspired
22 Adelaide St. West, 41st Floor
Toronto, Ontario M5H 4E3, Canada
www.LoveInspired.com

Printed in U.S.A.

Recycling programs for this product may not exist in your area.

Trust in the Lord with all thine heart; and lean not unto thine own understanding. In all thy ways acknowledge him, and he shall direct thy paths.
—*Proverbs* 3:5-6

This book is dedicated to the original Theo, air-scent dog extraordinaire Indiana Bones, and his handler, my sis-in-law Michelle. You two are an amazing team. And to my wonderful Suspense Squad. You ladies rock. I can't imagine doing this writing life without you.

ONE

Wednesday 1:00 p.m.

Trees towered above her, and dried shrubs threatened to entangle her feet. Marriage and family therapist and part-time search and rescue handler Charlotte Bradley jogged behind her air-scent dog, Theo. She hoped to find the missing girl she counseled at Sadie's Place, a home for pregnant teens who needed help.

Charlotte admired the girl's grit and struggled with the idea Hannah Davies had chosen to run away. There had to be more to her disappearance than simply an unhappy pregnant teen.

Theo had picked up Hannah's scent five minutes ago and had veered off into the woods, darting through the trees and brush. He'd now slowed and weaved back and forth, nose high in the air.

Charlotte's heart tumbled to her feet. She knew that movement. He'd lost the scent. "Theo, with me."

The dog plodded to her side and sat. She pulled

out a squeeze bottle to offer him a drink. Theo caught the stream of water in his mouth and gulped up the liquid.

When he'd had his fill, she stowed the bottle. "Well, handsome. What do you think?" Theo had caught the girl's scent and lost it three times now. Not a normal event for him. It was like Hannah had *poof* disappeared.

Charlotte placed her hand on Theo's head and scanned the area. What happened to the teen? No way Hannah had vanished into thin air. Charlotte just had to keep looking. That was all. The whole situation bothered her, but she couldn't put her finger on why. The concealed compact Glock resting at the small of Charlotte's back gave her a bit of comfort against the unease that stirred in her belly.

The smell of the impending snow drifted in the air, adding to her worry. The weatherman predicted a dumping of several feet of the white stuff. Not great timing. She inhaled and lifted her face to the sky. A prayer for holding off the storm came to mind, but she brushed it away. When was the last time God answered her prayers?

But maybe He'd answer one for Hannah.

A burst of an icy breeze whistled through the trees, halting her thoughts and sending a shiver racing through her body. She zipped her winter coat to her chin and adjusted her stocking hat. With a gloved hand, she patted Theo on the head.

"Come on, boy. She has to be here somewhere. *Find.*" Charlotte pushed back brush and ducked under bare tree limbs. Her boots crunched on the dried leaves as she followed Theo to a different section. She came across a narrow dirt path that twisted through the woods. Not much of a trail, but she'd take it. It sure beat the underbrush.

Seventeen-year-old Hannah Davies had disappeared twelve hours ago. Not enough time had passed for them to call in a normal search and rescue, but when the SAR coordinator discovered the girl was eight months pregnant, she'd sent Charlotte and Theo out along with three other search teams to hunt for Hannah. The sheriff's department had assigned men who knew the area, but they had no training in search and rescue other than basic skills. Command had partnered the volunteers with the experienced personnel. Not ideal, but with the short notice, she and her incident commander, Gayle, took what they could get. If only the other teams had scent dogs, they'd increase the likelihood of finding the teen by a lot, but no other SAR canine team was available.

Sunlight filtered through the bare trees and evergreens dotting the narrow trail. Streams of light reflected off the white on Theo's service-dog vest, giving him a sweet aura. Charlotte increased her pace, not willing to lose sight of him.

The dog had come to her four years ago as a gift that had more than likely saved her life. After the heart-wrenching loss of her baby, she'd absorbed Theo's love and spent the next few years training him as an air-scent canine. He'd learned fast and now ranked among the top SAR dogs in the region.

Theo slowed. His nose high in the air. "Do you have her?" She studied the English shepherd, waiting for him to continue. With air-scent dogs, time mattered. Scents only lasted so long, and if it rained or snowed, his ability to track the person diminished and quickly disappeared.

Theo took off, aiming deeper into the foliage. She jogged behind him, careful of her step. A twisted or broken ankle wouldn't help matters out here.

She unclipped the radio from her belt, keeping Theo in sight. "Team one to command."

"Go ahead, Charlotte."

"Theo has something in grid ten." Her voice wobbled with the exertion.

"Copy that."

"Thanks, Gayle." Since Charlotte had used her radio, the incident commander didn't need to relay the information to the others since they all used the same channel. Any private conversations came by way of her cell phone, which had spotty service out here. But they used the phones when they could. She clipped the radio back onto her belt and returned her focus to Theo.

The temperatures had dropped another five degrees over the last half an hour, and the clouds possessed an angry look that made Charlotte cringe. Time was not on her side.

Her cell phone dinged. She pulled it from her pocket and glanced at the text message.

Sheriff Monroe is on his way.

She'd met the local sheriff a couple of times and had also heard great things about him. She just hoped the man wouldn't stop the search due to the weather. They had to find Hannah.

Copy that.

Unsure whether to consider the news good or bad, Charlotte continued her hunt for the girl she'd come to care about over the past four months. As an MFT at Sadie's Place, she counseled pregnant teens. Her own experience brought a wealth of understanding to the girls. She'd *been there, done that,* and lost in the most horrible way. Now, she helped others deal with unexpected pregnancies and the decisions they faced.

Theo curved around a bush and dashed ahead. Charlotte picked up her pace to follow her dog around the foliage and came face-to-face with a low-hanging branch. She threw her arm up to protect herself a little too late and received a blow to her cheek that would leave a nice bruise.

The dog slowed, lifted his nose in the air, sat and gave a quick bark.

"What do you have?" She ducked under another branch, avoiding a matching bruise on her other cheek. Her heart sank. A hot-pink scarf dangled from a bush. One like Hannah wore. Charlotte crouched next to it and ran her fingers under the scarf.

She scanned the area. "Where are you, Hannah?"

A lump ten feet away snagged her attention.

"Hannah?" Charlotte pushed to a standing position. The hairs on her neck prickled. She drew her weapon, held it against her leg, and eased her way to the object. The nearer she got, the heavier the rock sat in the pit of her stomach. She glanced at Theo. He continued to sit next to the scarf. Odd. Charlotte steeled her spine and stepped closer. She looked down at her feet and sucked in a breath.

Blood pooled on the ground, and a medallion peeked through the crimson liquid. She raised her gun and forced her gaze to the large object in question.

Blood-covered legs protruded from the bush.

The discovery registered in her brain, and the world tilted, taking her to her knees.

Wednesday 3:00 p.m.

He couldn't catch a break today. Sheriff Dennis Monroe slammed the door of his department-issued SUV and plodded toward the SAR tent. He'd picked up his five-year-old daughter from school at noon and had planned to spend the rest of the day with her. He'd only met Amelia for the first time six months ago, and he tried to spend as much time as he could with his daughter. Unfortunately, his dispatcher, Annie, had called, and he'd scrambled to find someone to stay with Amelia so he could hurry to the trailhead.

"Afternoon, Gayle." He retrieved his gloves from his coat pocket and put them on. "Any word yet?"

The woman stood and smoothed the map on the table. "Charlotte called in a while ago. Her dog, Theo, was on to something."

A faint scream echoed through the woods.

Gayle sucked in a breath. "Charlotte."

"Where?" He placed his hands on the edge of the table and stared at the map.

Gayle pointed to a highlighted section. "Grid ten."

After a quick study of the location, he took off in the direction of the scream.

"You and me, channel two," Gayle yelled after him.

He waved an acknowledgment, adjusted his radio to channel two and settled into a quick jog. From what he remembered, Charlotte was a seasoned SAR volunteer. He'd met her two other times in passing, and the little he knew about Charlotte, he'd pegged her as levelheaded. Her reaction sent worst-case scenarios darting through his mind. Had she run into an animal like a coyote? Or was her response due to danger of the human variety?

His radio crackled. "Sheriff."

He unclipped the device from his belt. "Go ahead, Gayle."

"Charlotte found a body."

Dennis picked up his pace. "Is it Hannah Davies?"

"Unsure. Charlotte's maintaining her distance so that she doesn't compromise the scene."

"Good. I'm on my way." Dennis glanced at the darkening sky. "Tell the others to bring it in. I don't want anyone caught out in the storm that's coming."

"Copy that, Sheriff."

"Oh, and give Mel a call. Have her meet me at the scene."

"Coroner Melanie Hutton-Cooper. Got it."

"Thanks." He clipped the radio back on his belt and increased his speed another notch.

Fifteen minutes later, sweat beading on his forehead and breathing heavily, he rounded the corner and spotted Charlotte perched on a large rock. The woman sat snuggling what looked like a sixty-pound English shepherd.

He halted his progress, not wanting to startle her. "Ms. Bradley?"

She lifted her tearstained face and blinked. A purple bruise on her cheek stood out on her fair skin.

Dennis rushed to her side. "What happened? Do you need a medic?"

"No, no. I ran into a branch earlier, but I'm okay." She swiped the tears from her cheeks. "You're Sheriff Monroe, right?"

"Dennis. Please." He held out his hand, and she accepted the gesture.

"Nice to meet you. I'm Charlotte, and this is Theo." She ruffled the dog's fur. Her gaze drifted to an area less than ten feet away. "She's over there."

His heart dropped to his toes. Had Charlotte found the missing girl? "Is it Hannah?"

"I'm not sure. I saw bloody legs sticking out. I didn't want to get any closer, so I backtracked and stayed over here." Charlotte tightened her grip on Theo.

"I'm sorry you're the one who found her, but I appreciate you keeping the scene uncontaminated." Dennis peeled off his glove, extracted his phone from his pocket and snapped pictures before moving closer.

"Theo found Hannah's scarf over there." Charlotte pointed to the pink piece of cloth hanging from a bush.

Confusion swirled in Dennis's brain. Had he missed something? "Theo didn't alert to the body?"

She shook her head. "No. He's an air-scent dog, not a cadaver dog. He was searching for Hannah and alerted to her scent on the scarf. I just happened to find the body when I scanned the surroundings. Although, it's odd that he alerted to the scarf and not her. If it *is* her."

Dennis nodded, then crouched beside the dead woman. The air left his lungs, and the contents of his stomach almost followed. He swallowed the bile creeping up his throat.

"What is it?"

He glanced over his shoulder. Charlotte had stood but remained in her spot, hugging her waist.

He closed his eyes. How could he tell her about the gruesome scene in front of him? When he leveled his gaze on her, his heart ached at her defeated expression. "I'm not sure if it's the girl you're looking for, but I can tell you she *was* pregnant."

Her eyes widened. "Was?"

There were no words to cushion the blow. "Someone performed a crude C-section, and the baby is missing."

Of all the horrible things he'd seen in his career, this topped them all. He took a few more pictures for evidence and strode over to Charlotte. "Our county coroner, Dr. Melanie Hutton-Cooper, will be here in a little bit. Unfortunately, she volunteered to watch my daughter for me when I got the call-out. I'm sure she's making arrangements for another babysitter and will be here soon."

Charlotte worried her bottom lip. "You have a little girl?" she whispered.

"Yes." Her reaction struck him as peculiar. He tilted his head and studied her for a moment. "She keeps me busy, but I wouldn't have it any other way." The conversation was heading in a personal direction, and he didn't like it. Time to switch the focus. "Let me give Mel a call and get an ETA."

He stepped away and dialed Melanie's number.

"Hey, Sheriff." Mel's teasing tone made him smile. Her husband, Jason, was one of his four detectives and a good friend. In fact, all his detectives were in the same early to mid-thirty age range, which made being their boss challenging at times. And other times, they all gave him grief in a fun way, and Mel fit right in with the bunch.

"Did you find someone to stay with the princess?"

"Sure did. Amy and Keith are with her now. I'm on my way."

He relaxed a bit, knowing people he trusted were watching over his daughter. The transition from bachelor to single dad hadn't been easy, but he managed with the help of his church family and friends. "Good to know. Thanks for taking care of that. And, uh, Mel?"

"Yeah?"

"Be prepared." Melanie had seen worse, but the sight was shocking even for the most seasoned investigator.

Mel hesitated. "Understood. See you in about fifteen." The call disconnected.

Dennis stared at his phone for a long minute, then stuffed it into his pocket. He might as well see if the victim had ID on her while they waited. He slipped off his other snow glove and snapped on nitrile gloves.

"Please, stay right here, Ms. Bradley. I'll be back in a minute." He strode to the edge of the crime scene.

Careful not to disturb any evidence, he retraced his steps. He examined the victim's clothing for pockets and found none. With a trained eye, he assessed the area around the girl. No purse, phone or wallet. Maybe underneath her? But he'd let Mel move the body.

For now, all he could do was wait.

An arctic breeze chose that moment to zip through the trees and whip down his collar. He shivered and adjusted his coat.

The storm hovered on the outskirts of town and had caused darkness to descend early. It would be a race against the clock to collect evidence and retrieve the body before the weather destroyed all hope of finding anything that could help their investigation.

Dark clouds inched closer to Myers State Park. Charlotte's nerves danced on edge. She stared at the narrow dirt path, keeping her gaze away from the body she'd discovered.

Theo whined and nudged her hand.

She swallowed past the watermelon-size lump in her throat. "I'm okay, boy." Theo's warm fur beneath her fingers settled her racing heart. If the victim was Hannah—no, she couldn't go there—yet, who else could it be?

"Charlotte?" Dennis stepped beside her and pointed to a small boulder farther away from the scene. "There's a rock over there. Why don't you and Theo take a break? I know you've been out here searching for hours."

His words registered in her brain. Yes. She and Theo had worked for quite a while, and her dog needed water and a treat for finding the scarf. The object had given her hope until she'd stumbled across the woman in the shrubs.

Charlotte shuffled to the makeshift seat and plopped down. She unclipped the collapsible bowl, filled it with water from her bottle and placed it on the ground. Theo's black ears lifted, and he tilted his head, asking for permission. She rubbed his white-and-tan muzzle and traced the straight white line from his forehead down his snout. "You're a good boy, you know that, Theo?" She kissed his nose. "Go on, get a drink."

The dog lapped up the water, then bumped her leg.

She obliged his call for attention. She gave him a rope toy and played tug-of-war for a few minutes. Once they made it home, they'd play his favorite game of Frisbee. The pup would run himself silly and drop from exhaustion if she let him.

"Time's up, Theo." Charlotte tucked the rope into her backpack and pulled out a treat. Theo sat and waited to take the piece of dried chicken from her hand. "Okay."

The dog grabbed the snack from her fingers and devoured it. With play and snack time over, he lay down and placed his nose on her feet.

The breeze picked up, and the freezing air stung her cheeks, making the bruise she'd received earlier ache. She ducked her face into the neck of her insulated coat. Her gaze drifted to the body. How would she tell Hannah's parents?

"Yo, Sheriff," a female voice called from behind a copse of trees.

"Over here, Mel." Dennis moved next to Charlotte.

A petite brown-haired woman ducked under a branch, appeared and smiled. She must be the coroner the sheriff called. "Fancy meeting you here."

Dennis cleared his throat. "Mel, this is Charlotte Bradley, MFT and search and rescue volunteer. She and her SAR dog, Theo, found the victim. We're assuming it's her patient Hannah Davies."

Mel cringed. "Sorry about sounding so blasé. Occupational hazard." The woman stuck out her gloved hand.

Charlotte accepted the gesture and shook it. "No problem. I'm sure you see a lot of death."

"Yes, but you probably don't, especially when it's someone you know."

The sympathy in Dr. Hutton-Cooper's voice brought tears to Charlotte's eyes. "True."

"I see you found him." A tall blond man joined the small group. "You must be Charlotte. Name's Jason. I'm married to this beautiful woman, and I'm that lug's underling."

Dennis rolled his eyes. "Yes, and he's a little overdramatic."

"Who me?" Jason placed a hand over his heart. "Hurtful."

Dennis shook his head and turned his focus to her. "Charlotte, please excuse these two. I think the cold is affecting their manners."

Mel elbowed her husband in the gut.

"Hey." Jason rubbed the point of contact.

She jerked her head in Charlotte's direction.

Jason swung his gaze to her, and his eyes widened. "Sorry."

Charlotte shrugged. "It's okay." She'd worked with enough law enforcement during search and rescues that the easygoing banter and conversation didn't usually bother her. In fact, she joined in on occasion during difficult assignments, but today was different. The person she'd found was dead, and all signs pointed to it being Hannah. If only she'd had the nerve to look at the woman's face.

"Let me get to work and see if we can confirm the victim's identity." Mel stepped past Charlotte and approached the body. "Whoa."

Jason strode over and peered over Melanie's shoulder. "Oh, dude."

"Come on. Let's get to work." Melanie snapped on nitrile gloves and crouched next to the body. "Did Hannah have any birthmarks or tattoos that I should look for?"

Jason removed a camera from the kit he'd brought and started snapping pictures.

"She has a small butterfly tattoo on her left ankle." Charlotte rubbed her arms and watched Melanie remove the girl's shoe and sock. The woman examined the area that should sport the colorful tattoo.

"It's not Hannah."

Charlotte's knees buckled. Dennis's arm shot around her waist and held her upright. Theo nudged her and whined. She patted her dog on the head, hoping to ease his worry.

"Come here. Have a seat." Dennis guided her to the rock.

She lowered herself to the hard surface and closed her eyes. *It isn't Hannah.*

"Charlotte?"

The crunch of dirt, rock and leaves pulled her from the tunnel she'd fallen down when Melanie gave her the news. She blinked, clearing her muddled thoughts, and discovered a worried sheriff kneeling beside her.

Theo placed his paws on her lap and nosed her

neck. He wasn't a psychiatric service dog, but she'd taught him deep pressure stimulation to calm her when anxiety attacks struck. The dog had sensed her stress and responded. She buried her face in his fur and held him.

"He's amazing."

Charlotte inhaled and released Theo. "Good boy." She pulled a treat from her bag and gave it to her furry partner. "Down." Theo obeyed and lay at her feet. She turned her attention to Dennis. "He's…special." Funny, she believed in the existence of God but had no intention of giving Him credit for anything positive in her life—like Theo. God had let her down, and she continued to hold a grudge five years later.

Dennis tilted his head. A question wavered in his expression, but he refrained from asking. "You two make a great team."

"Thank you. I love helping people, and Theo was born for the job."

He motioned toward Theo. "May I pet him?"

She smiled. Someone who understood working dogs. Most people didn't realize that you shouldn't pet police, SAR or service dogs without asking. "Sure."

Dennis shifted and extended his hand, palm up.

Theo made eye contact with her. She nodded,

giving him permission to accept the attention from a stranger.

Theo's tail thumped on the ground in approval of the scratches behind the ears.

"He really is a great dog."

"One of the best air-scent dogs in the region. And my best friend."

When Dennis stood, she realized for the first time how handsome the local sheriff was—and how young. He looked to be around the same age as his deputy that had shown up with the coroner.

"Excuse me." Jason appeared by her side. "I'd like to see if you can identify the girl you found."

Her heart raced at an alarming speed. A hand rested on her arm, and she peered into the sheriff's unusual gray eyes.

"It's okay, Charlotte. Jason won't show you anything graphic." He pinned his deputy with a steely gaze.

"No, of course not. I have a picture of the girl's face. She has a couple of bruises, but nothing beyond that."

Come on, Charlotte. Get it together. She took three deep breaths to settle her pulse. "Let me see."

Jason turned the camera screen in her direction.

A strangled cry erupted from her. "Oh, no. It can't be."

"Who?" Dennis maneuvered to examine the image.

Charlotte covered her mouth, hoping her breakfast stayed put. "That's Stella. She's one of my girls."

"What do you mean?" Dennis asked.

"Stella's one of the teens from Sadie's Place. I've counseled her for the last three months." Tears dripped from her chin, leaving a freezing trail on her skin. Her mind scrambled to sort through the information. "I don't understand. Stella's dead, and her baby is missing. And Hannah has disappeared." She shifted her gaze to Dennis. "What's happening?"

Mel snapped off her nitrile gloves and joined them. "I overheard. I'm truly sorry for your loss."

"Thank you." Theo sat and stared at her, concern lacing his big brown doggy eyes. "Now what?"

"We need to figure out who did this to Stella and find Hannah." Dennis pivoted and faced Jason. "You and Mel take our victim to the lab and see what you can discover. Call Dr. Vogel, the ME, and tell him I want the autopsy A-SAP. And get Kyle Howard out here with a crime scene tech, and tell them to bag up all the evidence they can find."

"On it, boss." Jason pulled his cell phone from his pocket and moved away to place the call.

"Mel, I think I can make my own conclusions on the basics, but keep me updated on the autopsy when Dr. Vogel's done. And do me a fa⌐⌐⌐ and sit in on it."

"You got it. Dr. Doom won't like it, but I'll make sure I'm there." Mel rested a hand on Charlotte's shoulder. "I'll take good care of her."

Charlotte's gaze drifted to the petite woman. She couldn't find her voice, so she simply nodded her thanks.

"Charlotte and I will continue the search for Hannah, then I'll come help with the investigation." He glanced at her. "Assuming you're up for it."

"Yes, please. We have to find her."

Dennis glanced at the sky. "I don't like the look of those clouds, and we'll lose any light left soon. We're running out of time."

Her gaze followed his. The storm had moved faster than expected. They had maybe an hour before it hit.

Dennis gave his team last-minute instructions and checked his supplies.

Jason finished his phone call, and he and Mel went into a flurry of activity, prepping the body for transport.

Charlotte grabbed her pack, ready to resume the search. She waited on the rock with Theo by her side and chewed on her bottom lip.

What if they didn't find Hannah before the storm hit? A cold shiver snaked up her spine.

The bigger question: What if they were too late, and Hannah had already suffered the same demise as Stella?

Even after as many crime scenes as Dennis had experienced, he'd never forget the gruesomeness of what he'd just witnessed. His stomach continued to churn at the condition of the poor girl's body.

And the baby. Who took the infant? Did the father even know about the little life? His own past swooped in and stole the air from his lungs. He tore his gaze from the victim and forced the past where it belonged.

Dennis focused his attention on Charlotte. "Are you sure you're up for continuing the search for Hannah?"

Her gaze drifted to meet his. Sorrow and pain poured from her. The strong desire to gather her in his arms jolted him. After his ex-girlfriend, Tina, turned his life upside down, he'd vowed to be careful where he put his interest when it came to women.

"I don't have a choice but to keep moving." Charlotte glanced at the sky. "We have to find Hannah before it's too late."

"I'm ready when you are." Dennis had complete confidence in Jason and Mel to take care of things here. Plus, Kyle was on his way to help.

The weather worried him on two fronts: the evidence at the crime scene and a pregnant teen out there in freezing temperatures. Dennis stretched his neck from side to side, relieving the tension rolling across his shoulders.

Backpack on, Charlotte tapped the small of her back. He recognized the motion of confirming that a weapon remained secure in a concealed holster. He'd done it many times himself over his career in law enforcement. After completing the check, Charlotte snapped her fingers, and Theo came to attention. She clipped on the dog's leash and faced Dennis. "We're ready."

He nodded and led the way through the brush and trees to the main trail. Once the path widened, Charlotte walked next to him.

Never letting his guard down, Dennis maintained a visual sweep of the area. A body and a missing girl had his "spidey" senses on high alert. He itched to find Hannah and get Charlotte out of here and to safety. He hoped the dog's abilities were as good as advertised.

"So how does this work?"

"Theo, *sit*." She moved to the dog, unclipped his leash, and pulled out a plastic bag containing a shirt. "This is one of Hannah's. I have him sniff it to get the scent, then I let him do his job."

He'd watched SAR dogs work before, but never up close with the handlers. The process would be fascinating if not for the missing girl. "All right, Theo, let's see how that amazing nose of yours works."

"You jest, but he's one of the best." Charlotte smiled at her dog, then opened the bag holding the piece of clothing. "*Check.*"

Theo sniffed the garment. Tail wagging, he waited for a command.

Charlotte stuffed the bag into her pack and knelt in front of the dog, staring eye to eye with him. "*Find.*"

Nose in the air, the dog got down to business. He took off along the trail, his head and tail held high.

"And now we follow." Charlotte picked up her pace.

Dennis blinked at the pair's quick response and hurried to catch up.

The group had jogged for five minutes when Theo came to a halt. He sniffed the air and paced back and forth.

Charlotte tilted her head and narrowed her eyes at a small grove of trees to the left of the trail. She held her palm up, fingertips pointing to that section. "*Check.*"

The dog headed toward the area and gave it a look.

"That'll do."

Theo pranced back and sat at her feet. She bit

the end of her glove, tugged it from her hand and gave him a treat from the pouch on her hip. "Good boy. Want a drink?" She took out a bottle and squeezed water at Theo's mouth. The dog caught the water in the air.

Dennis crossed his arms and smiled. "That was fun to watch."

"He loves his squeeze bottle." Charlotte stowed the bottle, and after replacing the glove, she ran a hand over Theo's head.

Curiosity killed Dennis. He couldn't figure out why Theo had paused in this spot. Had the dog alerted to something in the area? He couldn't contain the question any longer. He had to ask. "Why did Theo stop here?"

Charlotte adjusted her pack and shrugged. "I'm not sure. I wish I knew what he was thinking, but I trust him to get the job done. He's exceptional at what he does." She drew in a deep breath and released it. *"Find again."*

Once again, Dennis found himself following the black, white and brown dog down the trail. He glanced at the darkening sky. They had to find Hannah before night fell and the storm hit. If not… He refused to go there.

Dread settled in his belly, and an odd sensation blanketed him. His hand instinctively hovered over his holstered weapon, and he scanned the edges of the trail.

Theo took a right and darted into the woods twenty yards ahead. He jogged next to Charlotte and followed the dog into the thick brush.

"He's caught the scent of something." Dennis let Charlotte lead the way.

"Yes. I'm just hoping he finds Hannah soon." A white swirl of breath rose from her mouth as she spoke.

Dennis ducked under a low-hanging limb and dodged a snarl of vines lying on the ground. The dog knew how to pick rugged terrain.

"You said you have a daughter?" Charlotte's breathy words caught him off guard.

Small talk? Now? He hoped not to break an ankle, and she wanted to chitchat.

"Sorry. I'm trying to keep my mind from conjuring up worst-case scenarios."

A fat snowflake splatted on his cheek. Then another and another. He swiped his gloved hand across his face. She had to mention worst-case.

"Yes. She's five years old, and her name is Amelia." He heard a muffled gasp from Charlotte but decided not to acknowledge it and continued to praise his little girl. Someone needed to after her rough start in life. "She's quite the character. We've worked hard on behavior issues, but man, is she smart. She's only in kindergarten and is already reading chapter books. It's amazing, really."

"You and her mother must be proud."

He snorted. "As if." That was a story in and of itself, and one he'd like to forget. Why had he opened up to this woman?

Charlotte glanced over her shoulder at him with a raised eyebrow.

He toyed with how much to tell her. He'd officially met her a little while ago and had no reason to spill the details, so he'd go with the basics. "I found out about Amelia six months ago when her mother died."

Charlotte's gaze snapped to him, and her mouth gaped. "You didn't know?"

"It's a long story, but no. Her mother never told me."

"I shouldn't have said anything."

"No, it's okay. Tina was my ex-girlfriend years ago before I moved back to Valley Springs and became the sheriff."

And she lied to me that she'd miscarried our baby and then kept my kid from me for five years.

He'd had no idea that Tina had gone so far off the rails and into the world of drugs after she'd left him until he'd gotten *that* call.

Every time he thought about what his daughter experienced at the hands of her drug-addict mother, his blood pressure shot to new highs. He continued through the forest, letting his anger bleed away with the physical exertion.

Charlotte seemed to sense his need for quiet and quit talking as they continued the trek through the woods.

Dennis spotted the white on Theo's coat up ahead. "Man, he can run."

She chuckled. "He loves it. I have a big fenced-in yard, and he races the cars on the street."

A crack echoed through the air.

Dennis yanked his gun from his holster, grabbed Charlotte's arm and tugged her near a tree. He scanned the woods. Where had the gunshot come from?

"Theo, *now*!"

The dog raced back and fell in beside Charlotte. Another shot rang out, and a chunk of bark splintered mere inches from Dennis's temple. He pushed Charlotte's head down and grabbed his radio.

"Shots fired. Finding safety." A specific location wasn't an option on an open channel. He prayed his deputies knew him well enough to determine where he'd head.

Dennis itched to go after the shooter, but he had no choice; he had to get Charlotte and Theo out of danger.

He jerked on her sleeve and pulled her with him. "Come on. Let's go."

TWO

Two more bullets zinged past. Charlotte paused, and Dennis halted next to her with his weapon drawn. She snapped on Theo's leash. Out of duty, Theo would stand and protect her, but she refused to let him get hurt if she could prevent it.

"*With me,*" she commanded, and Theo ran alongside her. She cringed at the noise level of their footfalls that were no doubt alerting the attacker to their location.

"This way." Dennis held a branch aside, and she ducked under.

Wood splintered to her left and caught her cheek, sending a warm trickle down her face. She swiped at it, leaving a red streak on her glove.

"You okay?"

"Just peachy." She itched to yank her weapon from her concealed holster, but the way her hands shook, she had no business holding a gun right now. Besides, Dennis had *her* back, and she had Theo's.

He placed his hand on her back and urged her forward. The snowfall increased, and she blinked away the moisture on her lashes. Each passing minute made it challenging to see more than five or ten feet ahead.

Bullets continued to pepper across their path.

The cold stung her lungs, and her muscles quivered. She silently pleaded for the onslaught to end. The sound of Dennis's breathing comforted her. Knowing she wasn't alone gave her hope.

"Where are we going?" Charlotte couldn't hold on much longer. Her body begged her to stop. She and Theo had already searched for hours and were exhausted, but she'd push through to protect her dog.

"Let's circle around and work our way back to the command post. If that's not an option, I have another place in mind." Dennis grabbed her hand and tugged her through a grove of trees.

"Sounds like a plan, as long as the storm doesn't get worse."

Seconds later, the sky turned an angry dark gray, and a frigid breeze blew in. The snowstorm hit full force, dumping snow at an alarming rate, turning the world around her white.

"You had to say it."

"Sorry. Now what?"

Dennis pulled her behind a bush. "Secondary location. We have to get out of this. With visibility this bad, I'm afraid we'll run right into the man with the gun if we keep going. Or get so lost we end up freezing to death."

"What a lovely image. Thanks a lot." The man really knew how to paint a grim picture.

His gray eyes peered at her through the blanket of white. "Just keeping it real."

"I know. I get sassy when I'm scared." She could have sworn she heard him chuckle.

"I know a place we can hide until the weather eases."

Wet flakes hit her face, and the freezing wind threatened to sneak into her clothes. She tightened her grip on Theo's leash. "Lead on."

Her foot struck a rock, and she pitched forward. Strong arms caught her before she hit the ground.

"Are you okay?"

"Yes. Keep going." A safe place to stop and rest couldn't come soon enough. She ducked her head and plodded behind Dennis.

"There. Just ahead." He pointed at… What? A snowy mass of rock?

She wiped her eyes and squinted but still didn't see it. "Where?"

"There's a small rocky indention. Kind of like a shallow cave."

"If you say so." Charlotte's steps slowed as the snow accumulated. "Did you notice the shooting stopped?"

"For now."

"Aren't you just a ball of encouragement." She decided right then that if she got sassy when scared, sarcasm was Dennis's coping mechanism.

He huffed and trudged along the edge of a rock wall. "It should be here somewhere."

"You don't know?" He had to be kidding. The temperature could kill them, and he was guessing? Great.

"It's hard to find with all the snow."

That was a plus. If they had problems finding it, so would the man shooting at them.

"There." He pointed.

She followed his gesture. Sure enough, a well-hidden opening under the rocky overhang greeted them. Dennis led the way inside and to the back wall.

"Have a seat."

Charlotte dropped to the ground, and Theo lay beside her, panting in her lap. She ran a hand over his head. She'd give him water and food in a minute, but first she had to catch her breath.

Dennis slipped off his backpack, strode to the entrance and peered out.

His actions sent her pulse racing. "Is there a problem?"

He turned to face her. "Other than someone trying to kill us?" He rubbed his forehead with the back of his glove. "I'm sorry. I'm usually not so grumpy."

"I get it." She tilted her head and studied him. As sheriff, Dennis had to be used to tense situations. So why did the man look like a rubber band ready to snap? "Did the man follow us?"

"Not that I know of."

"Then what's wrong? Is there something else going on that you want to talk about? I'm a good listener."

He pursed his lips, and his chest rose and fell. The man remained silent. Nope, he had no intention of sharing. It didn't take a degree in psychology to figure that out.

She shook her head and shoved her fear aside. Her partner needed tending to. She pulled a water bottle, collapsible dog bowl and unsalted beef jerky from her pack. Theo deserved her attention. The poor pup had worked hard all day and had to be thirsty and hungry.

Charlotte served her furry friend. While her dog consumed the offered meal, she rested her head back against the rock wall and closed her eyes. She was stuck in a makeshift cave with someone shooting at her, plus she'd found a body and Hannah was still missing. She released a long breath.

She knew better than to ask, but what else could happen?

What was wrong? Everything.

Dennis reached for his radio and stopped. He had to call in soon, but it was rude not to answer Charlotte's question. He turned to the opening and continued his scan of the area.

Get out of your head, dude. It's not Charlotte's fault you're out here. She doesn't deserve your attitude.

The temperatures had dropped, and the snow continued to fall, creating a whiteout. Dennis had used the storm and shooter as an excuse for his grumpiness, but it was time to man up.

He turned and found Theo snacking and Charlotte resting against the rock. Might as well admit what had him in a snit. "I'm worried about my daughter."

Charlotte's eyes opened. "Didn't you say someone is watching her?"

"Yes. But I'm concerned she'll think I've abandoned her." His greatest fear was that Amelia wouldn't trust him to be there when she needed him.

Charlotte tilted her head and raised a brow.

He sighed. He'd started the conversation, he

might as well finish. "After her momma left me for another man, she started doing drugs. And from what I've discovered, she left Amelia alone a lot so she could go get high with her boyfriend."

"That's terrible."

The thought of his little girl fending for herself at such a young age squeezed his heart. "When her momma died, the boyfriend wanted nothing to do with her. He told the police Amelia wasn't his and to give her to her father." He blinked back tears. "Thankfully, my ex told the guy the whole story. He knew my name, and child protective services found me."

"Oh, Dennis." Pain filled her expression.

He nodded. "I thank God every day for my baby girl. But what her momma did…"

"That's why you're worried about leaving her."

"Yes." He strived to maintain a routine. Even with his odd hours at times, Amelia knew what to expect. Today was an anomaly in the structure he'd worked so hard to create.

"It couldn't have been easy becoming an instant father to a five-year-old."

"It wasn't. Isn't. But I've vowed to make her a priority, and my friends and coworkers support that." Blessed. The only word that described how he felt about having the community behind him and Amelia.

"Can you call her from in here?" Charlotte waved her hand at the interior of the cave.

"No service, but I plan to contact the others in a minute." He tapped his radio on his leg. "First, I wanted to make sure no one followed us, but I can't see a thing out there. How are you and Theo?"

"We're good. I need to do a medical check. Look him over and check his paws, but I figured food and water were on the top of Theo's list." She smiled and hugged the dog's neck. "Go on. We're fine. Do what you need to do."

"Thanks." Dennis slid to the ground beside Charlotte, unholstered his weapon and laid it beside his leg. Time to radio in an update and request help. "Monroe to base."

"Base here. Hey, boss."

"Jason. Did you and Kyle get the body and evidence out before the snow dumped?"

"Sure did. Are you guys okay? We heard the gunshots."

"Yeah, we're fine. For now." Dennis relayed what had happened. "We found a place to tuck in until the storm passes and wait for you to come find us."

"Good idea. I looked at the forecast. It's supposed to last several more hours."

Just as he'd suspected. "It'll get cold, but we've got shelter, and food and water in our packs." The freezing temps worried him more than the gunman at this point.

"Other than watching out for the shooter and informing the other deputies, what can I do *for you*?" Jason's tone turned serious.

Relief flooded him at Jason's offer. "Please check on Amelia. Tell her that I'll be home as soon as I can." Man, he hated leaving her without talking to her first. But with his cell phone coverage at zero, what choice did he have?

"Mel and I are on it. Maybe we'll go have a movie night with her."

"No sugar, or you'll be up all night."

"And what's the problem with that?" His friend was incorrigible.

Dennis rolled his eyes. "Go ahead. Let's see how you feel about it in the morning."

Jason laughed. "Seriously, man, we've got your daughter covered. She'll feel loved."

His friend understood, and he had complete faith that Jason and the rest would do their best. But it wasn't the same as being there to tuck her in himself. He owed it to Amelia to make her life stable. "Thanks, Jason."

"Anytime. You know that."

And he did. "Still…" He let the implied meaning hang in the air.

"Got it. We'll send out a search party to rescue the search party when the weather clears. Jason out."

Chuckles filtered through the line before it went silent. Dennis laid the radio on the ground and glanced at his cell phone one more time. No bars. The rocks and weather were playing havoc with the cell service. He stuffed it back into his pocket.

The cold ground seeped through his pant legs, sending a chill through him. At least his daughter was safe and warm with a full tummy. More than she'd experienced in the first few years of her life.

The dagger of hurt twisted in his chest. If only he'd known about her. Why Tina had lied to him about having a miscarriage, he'd never know.

A small, gloved hand rested on his. "She'll be all right."

He looked at Charlotte. She sat snuggled with a sleeping Theo. At least the dog would keep her warm. He shrugged and nodded. "Sure." No, he wasn't sure, but he had to trust his friends and God. "Go ahead and get some sleep. I'll keep watch."

Her shoulders sagged, and a flash of hurt filled her eyes, then disappeared. "Thanks."

Dennis had done it again. He'd hurt her feelings. He rose, slipped his gun back into his holster and stomped to the entrance. He stood just inside the makeshift cave, out of the falling snow and away from the biting wind.

No way was the shooter still out there, but he refused to take any chances. He wouldn't leave his daughter an orphan. Plus, he had a woman and dog to protect. Failure to do his job meant people died. He wouldn't fail.

A boom echoed through the tiny cave.

Dennis snapped to attention and yanked his weapon from the holster. "Stay here!"

He sprinted out into the storm, leaving Charlotte and Theo's safety in God's hands.

THREE

Theo popped up. His fur bristled, and he released a guttural growl. The dog shot off toward the opening. Charlotte grabbed for his collar to keep him from charging out into the storm after Dennis but missed.

"Theo!"

The dog disappeared into the white beyond the cave entrance.

Charlotte charged after him but stopped short of leaving the protection of the rocky den. She lifted her arm to protect her face from the gusts of wind stirred up by the increasing storm and strained to hear Theo and Dennis, but reality set in. She was on her own, and the man who'd risked his life to protect her was nowhere to be found.

She moved farther into the shelter and braced her back against the rock wall. A lump formed in her throat as she slid to the ground. Could Theo find his way back to the makeshift cave? What would she do if she lost her dog forever?

Tears trickled down her cheeks, warming her skin then leaving an ice-cold path. The stark contrast, an example of her life. Happy times shadowed by tragedy. One more loss in her life seemed apropos.

Uncertain how long she sat with her arms wrapped around her bent knees, she rested her head on the rock behind her and accepted reality. Dennis and Theo weren't coming back. There was no way they'd survived the ferocity of the storm.

Doing what she'd vowed five years ago not to do, she reached out to God for help. *Now what, God? I have no way to call for help. Do I go out and try to find them?*

For Theo, she'd risk everything. The dog had saved her at the lowest point in her life. She'd forever be grateful. Charlotte had to try. Decision made, she stood.

A bark caught her attention.

She straightened. Theo?

Another bark, then another. Theo's black nose peeked from beneath a layer of snow on his coat. Dennis held Theo's collar and stumbled in behind her dog.

Charlotte rushed to Dennis's side. He released the collar and swayed. She wrapped her arm around his waist and took some of his weight. When he staggered, she tightened her grip.

"Come on. Let's get you sitting down before you fall down."

"Thanks." His teeth chattered, and his body shook.

She lowered him to the ground and brushed the snow from his face. "Hold on." She unzipped her pack and retrieved two towels.

SAR teams teased her about including towels in her supplies. They claimed she treated Theo like a prince when she wiped him down after he trailed through creeks or rain. Right now, she was glad she had them. She'd keep one towel for her four-legged friend, but the other had Dennis's name on it.

"Let's dust some of this snow off, then we'll work on getting you warmed up."

He hugged his middle and nodded.

She started with his face and head, then moved down to his arms and chest. His blue lips and red skin worried her. Charlotte yanked the thin wool blanket she included for Theo to lie on from her pack and pulled the survival blanket from Dennis's.

"I'm going to wrap you in the wool blanket first, then add the Mylar one on top."

"Th-anks." His words slurred, and his eyes drooped.

Not good.

Hypothermia had edged in, and she had to increase his body temperature—fast. She tucked the material around him, then dug into her bag again for the instant hot packs. After activating the heat, Charlotte stuffed one into each of Dennis's gloves and put the large one inside the blanket next to his chest. Now that she had Dennis taken care of, she turned her attention to Theo. After a good rubdown, Theo ambled over to Dennis and lay across his lap.

The cold seeped into her clothes and sent a shiver up her spine and into her scalp. She tugged her hat tighter on her head and took inventory of their shelter. Not much to help her situation, but—were those twigs on the other side? She crawled over and breathed a sigh of relief. There weren't many, but enough to make a fire to warm up Dennis and dry out Theo's fur and possibly last hours if she rationed the sticks. The fire wouldn't be big, but any heat would help.

She tossed a handful of twigs along with a few dried leaves into a pile a few feet from a sleeping Dennis and Theo. Charlotte stuck a fire-starter stick under the wood and flicked on the lighter she kept for emergencies. The wax at the end of the starter caught fire and crawled across the surface, igniting the leaves. A few minutes later, the twigs took hold and crackled. Flames danced in the air, and the smoke floated to the entrance and out into the night. Warmth drifted from the tiny fire, giving her a bit of relief from the dropping temperatures.

Her gaze wandered to Dennis. Theo's eyes opened, and he tilted his head.

"It's okay, boy. Go back to sleep."

The dog released a sigh and rested his head on his front paws.

Collecting the remaining pile of twigs and small branches became her focus. The fire might alert someone of their location, but without it, they would all freeze to death. So she'd take the risk.

Charlotte tended the flames over the next six hours and waited for Dennis to wake up.

When he'd come back impersonating the abominable snowman, she'd worried about hypothermia. But thanks to the tiny fire, his skin had lightened to pink and he'd stopped shivering.

She tossed another two small pieces of wood on the fire and watched it crackle.

With a sigh, she checked her watch again and prayed he'd wake up soon. Sitting in a rocky den in a snowstorm was bad enough, but the situation gave her too much time to think about all she'd lost and worry about Hannah.

The howling wind through the entrance sent the fine hairs on the back of her neck standing straight. She slid her Glock from under her back-pack and placed it on her leg. Charlotte hoped the storm let up soon and help arrived before the bad guy found them or they froze to death.

The faint smell of smoke wafted through the cave, tingling Dennis's senses, pulling him from his sleep. His body ached, and a chill had settled into his bones. He shifted, but a heavy weight pressed on his legs. Dennis swallowed the fear and searched his mind for what had happened.

A frozen branch had snapped. He'd rushed from the makeshift cave thinking the madman had returned and fired a weapon at their hiding place. It had taken all of thirty seconds to realize nature had caused the commotion. He'd turned back toward the cave to rejoin Charlotte and her dog, but a second branch had snapped and fallen to the ground, trapping him in the deepening snow.

Funny, he didn't feel frozen. Cold, yes, but not Popsicle-worthy.

"Dennis." A soft voice penetrated his foggy brain.

He blinked and searched his surroundings. Three rock walls and an open mouth at one end. The smallest fire he'd ever seen wavered in his vision. His gaze landed on the source of the weight on his legs. Theo. He closed his eyes and thumbed through his memories.

If it hadn't been for Theo, Dennis would've frozen to death. The dog had nudged him and pulled on the sleeve of his jacket. He wasn't sure how the dog had done it, but Theo had saved his life.

He ran his hand over the dog's fur when a sloppy wet tongue licked his fingers. "Thank you, Theo."

"He's pretty amazing, isn't he?" A hand rested on his arm. He looked up into the sweetest brown eyes he'd ever seen. "Charlotte?"

"I'm here. How are you feeling?" She ran the back of her hand across his forehead.

"Thanks to Theo here, I'm alive." He owed the dog his life. After Theo had helped him from under the limb, Dennis had grabbed his collar and Theo had led him back to the shelter. The last thing Dennis remembered was collapsing against the wall. "Would you mind filling in the pieces after Theo brought me back?"

"I dried you and Theo off the best I could and wrapped you up in the wool blanket from my pack."

"Apparently, you're a boy scout." He gestured toward the flames.

"Yeah, let's go with that." She chuckled. "I had to warm you up, so I took a risk and made a fire."

Dennis glanced at her lap and spotted her gun. "Did something happen?"

She shook her head. "No. I hate to admit it, but I got spooked."

"With all that's happened, I'm not surprised." Guilt flooded his system. "How long was I out?"

Charlotte tilted her head and pinched her lips together. "About six hours."

He sat stunned by the news. "You have to be kidding me?"

"You weren't in good shape when you came back. I thought for sure hypothermia had sunk in its teeth and you'd never make it until help arrived."

He swiped a hand down his face. Reality punched him in the gut. Not only would he have left Charlotte unprotected, his daughter would have become an orphan. He owed God a big thank-you.

"The snow has stopped." Charlotte interrupted his thoughts. "How soon do you think it'll be before they find us?"

"I'm not sure. It depends on how passable the trails are. It'll be daylight before they try." He glanced at the fire and sent up a prayer that it lasted until help arrived.

The two oscillated between quiet and small talk while Theo snored. Several hours later, the radio crackled with static.

"Sheriff, do you copy?"

Dennis reached for the device and regretted the movement but wrapped his fingers around the lifeline and answered. "I copy. What's the word, Jason?"

"It'll take us a bit to get to you. The storm dumped a lot of white stuff."

"I'm assuming you know where you're going?" Dennis prayed his friends knew him well enough that he wouldn't have to give away their location over an open channel.

"Let me see. I'm thinking you took a wrong turn at Albuquerque."

Dennis shook his head. Jason and his ridiculous cartoon reference. "Just come get us."

His deputy's voice turned serious. "Anyone need medical attention?"

He was about to respond when Charlotte snatched the radio from his hand.

"Jason, have an EMT waiting. The sheriff needs to be checked out."

"I do not." He retrieved the radio. "Ignore that."

"No can do, boss man. She's search and rescue. She knows what she's talking about."

"Insubordination doesn't become you, Deputy Cooper." Since when did his deputies take instructions from others?

"Deal with it, Dennis." Jason's tone turned serious, and the use of his first name changed everything.

"All right, you win." Who was he kidding? His back ached, and his body temperature hovered just above ice-cube level.

"See ya soon, boss." Jason's final words a promise under the man's easygoing tone.

"Do they even know where we are?"

A smile pulled at his lips. "Jason knows."

"How can you be so sure?"

"Because he didn't ask."

Her brow furrowed. The confusion on her face made him chuckle.

"Don't worry, my friends and I hike out here frequently. He knows where to find us. The cavalry will be here soon."

She opened her mouth as if to say something, then closed it. He could almost see the wheels turning inside her head. She picked up two out of the six remaining sticks and tossed them on the tiny fire. "How long do you think it'll take them?"

Dennis shifted to face Charlotte and groaned. Okay, so maybe he did need to see a medic. The bruise on his back throbbed. "I'm guessing thirty to forty minutes." He pointed to the burning twigs. "Think it'll last that long?"

She shrugged. "I hope so, but if not, it served its purpose and kept you alive through the night."

Theo stood and stretched, then plodded to Charlotte, flopped down and to rested his snout on her leg. Dennis instantly missed the dog's warmth. Probably one more reason he'd survived the experience.

He leaned his head against the rock wall and thanked God for sparing his life. Amelia's face wavered in his mind. He had no intention of leaving his daughter without a father.

"Are you doing okay?" Charlotte's question broke through his agonizing thoughts.

"Just thinking about Amelia." The two of them fell silent. But worry wouldn't help things. Dennis rubbed his hand up and down his thighs. Man, he missed Theo as a blanket. "Tell me about Hannah."

Charlotte's hand paused mid stroke on Theo's head. "What about her?"

"Why would she run away?"

"I don't think she would. Not for the reasons everyone assumes." She continued to stroke the dog's fur. "I was—and am—convinced something happened that scared her. Especially now that we found Stella."

"You said *was*. Why?" That made no sense to him. There was no evidence that suggested Hannah's disappearance was more than a scared pregnant teen that wanted to get away.

Charlotte eyed the dimming flames and bit her lower lip. He waited, unsure whether to push for an answer or let her mull over what she wanted to say.

"She was happy."

"Charlotte. You're a therapist. That's the least professional opinion I've ever heard."

"But it's true. I can analyze data. I can note symptoms and make a diagnosis, but I can't ignore the simplicity of the human factor. Yes, Hannah was scared and ashamed of her actions, but she and her parents were finally working their way back to good terms, not to mention she had the support of her boyfriend."

"Okay, so she was happy. What else?"

A crease deepened on her forehead. "She planned to give her baby a future with adoptive parents. But—"

"But what?"

"She told me last week she was having second thoughts and wanted to be a mom. As far as I know, she hadn't changed her mind, only toyed with the idea." Charlotte shrugged. "I don't know. Maybe I'm seeing things that aren't there."

A crunch from outside echoed through the mini cave.

Dennis's hand flew to his weapon. He raised it and aimed at the entrance. He noticed Charlotte had done the same.

Theo stood and braced his front paws in a defensive stance. A growl rumbled from him.

"Easy, Theo." Charlotte's calm tone surprised Dennis. The woman had nerves of steel. He'd give her that.

A head peeked around the corner ten feet away. "Hey, boss. Whoa. Don't shoot your rescuer." Jason moved inside, followed by Kyle.

"Hey, Sheriff. Need some help?" Kyle grinned.

Just what Dennis needed, a couple of class clowns. "Glad you're here." He stumbled to his feet, and a groan slipped from his lips.

Jason rushed over and ducked under his arm, steadying him before he face-planted. "Easy there, buddy."

"I'm good. Just stiff, that's all." He hoped he made it down the trail without making a liar out of himself.

"Sure. Let's go with that." Jason rolled his eyes. "How about we get you two out of here?"

"Sounds like a wonderful idea to me. I'm ready to get warm." Charlotte gathered her things and stomped out the fire while Kyle took care of Dennis's pack. She clipped on Theo's leash and straightened. "Ready when you are."

Jason leaned next to Dennis's ear. "Can you make it down the trail?"

Could he? He lowered his voice. "Do I have a choice?"

"Not unless you want me to throw you over my shoulder and fireman carry you out of here."

"That's what I was afraid of." He felt Jason's shoulders jiggle. The man was enjoying himself a little too much at Dennis's expense. Dennis turned his focus to Charlotte. "Let's get moving."

She nodded and followed an armed and alert Kyle out into the new fallen snow.

If not for Jason, Dennis would have smacked the ground within his first two steps. But his friend walked beside him, never letting him fall. Jason was like that. A man who always had his friends' backs.

For the next fifteen minutes, even with the rising sun glistening off the snow, Dennis focused on putting one foot in front of the other and ignored the beauty around him. His muscles had loosened, and his movements became more natural with each step. He sighed in relief that he'd make it to the trailhead without Jason making good on his promise of carrying him.

Now that his focus wasn't on staying upright, he shifted his attention to his deputy leading the way and smiled. Kyle's head was on a constant swivel. He held his weapon at his side, ready to intervene if danger came their way. His men were not only good friends but excellent deputies.

"By the way, Amelia thinks you had an adventure without her. She's convinced you stayed in an ice castle and didn't include her." Jason said.

"Watched *Frozen* last night, did you?"

Jason pursed his lips and glowered at him.

Dennis laughed and groaned. "It's her favorite. You know, Olaf reminds me of you."

"Thanks a lot, man. That snowman is ridiculous."

"Like I said." He cleared his throat to hide his chuckle.

Theo stopped in his tracks.

Dennis and Jason almost bumped into the back of Charlotte. All three drew their weapons. He and Jason scanned the area.

"What is it?" he asked.

"Not sure, but Theo isn't happy." Charlotte's weapon remained at her side, but she'd drawn it like everyone else.

"Come on, I want you out of here and somewhere safe." Dennis had no idea what the dog sensed, but he knew it was time to get moving.

The group picked up the pace. No one talked. Their attention remained on the surrounding woods.

A shiver climbed Dennis's neck and tingled his scalp.

He had a bad feeling that the threat to Charlotte was far from over.

FOUR

After sitting in the back of the ambulance for thirty minutes while they warmed him up and checked his injuries, Dennis made his way to his SUV, slid behind the steering wheel and relaxed into the seat. His back ached, and his head throbbed in time with his heartbeat.

"I don't like it." Brent, his friend and paramedic, held the SUV door open for him. "You should really go to the hospital."

"Advice noted."

"But you aren't going to take it, are you?" Brent huffed.

"Nope." His daughter was at home, and he needed to hold her in his arms. "Amelia's waiting."

"I get it. But if the pain gets worse, you'll go see the doc?"

"You have my word." Dennis extended his arm

to close the door, but Brent beat him to it, then strolled back to the ambulance.

Dennis sighed and cranked the engine. Even after all the blankets Brent and Ethan had covered him with, he was chilled to the bone. He flipped the heater on high and prayed it got hot soon.

Since Charlotte lived out of town, she'd agreed to head to his place to clean up before they headed out to question Hannah's boyfriend. The young man had to know more than he'd admitted to the officers when the search started for Hannah. Besides, the situation had changed with Stella's death. They had to reinterview anyone with a connection to either girl.

Dennis maneuvered through the parking lot and headed to the highway. He glanced in the rearview mirror and confirmed Charlotte had followed.

Twenty minutes later, he pulled into the driveway of his olive green craftsman-style house with cream trim and killed the engine. He'd bought the four-bedroom place in hopes of someday finding a wife and having children. Little did he know that he'd have the child but not the wife to go with the dream.

Pain still surfaced when he thought of all the years he'd missed with Amelia, and how his little girl had suffered during that time. He rested his head on the steering wheel, letting the physical and emotional pain wash through him. How could Tina have done that to him and their daughter?

A knock on the driver's window startled him. He glanced up and found Charlotte staring at him. Concern and something else filled her brown eyes. Fear? No. Uncertainty maybe.

He opened the door, and the cold air slapped him in the face. He slid from the seat, hoping his legs held his weight. His girl was inside, and more than anything in the world, he needed her in his arms. Hands on the door frame to brace himself, he let his body adjust before ambling toward the house. "Come on. Let me introduce you to my daughter."

Charlotte's steps faltered for a split second. If he hadn't been watching her at that moment, he would've never known that it had happened.

The small set of stairs to the front door looked like a mountain. He sucked in a breath, gathered his remaining bit of energy, and plodded up the steps. He let Charlotte and Theo in the house and closed the door behind him.

"Daddy!" Amelia came tearing around the corner and threw herself into his outstretched arms.

Dennis grunted at the impact, but he'd take a million more bruises to have his daughter safe in his arms.

Her tiny hands trapped his face. She tilted her head. "Uncle Jason said you were stuck in the storm and couldn't get home. Is that true?"

The seriousness in her voice made his heart shatter. She'd experienced more than any child should, but he'd vowed never to lie to her. His answers might be age-appropriate, but they were always the truth.

"Yes. I found shelter though and waited out the storm. But now I'm here."

She stared into his eyes like a little lie detector, then nodded. "I'm happy you're home. Aunt Amy said I could be late to school."

Amy, the wife of his deputy Keith Young, came from the kitchen, wiping her hands on a towel. "I hope that's okay with you."

"More than. I'd hoped I'd get to see my princess before she left for kindergarten." He tucked Amelia in for another hug and mouthed *thank you* to Amy. He pulled back and placed his hands on his daughter's shoulders. "There's someone I'd like you to meet."

As if the world opened around them, Amelia glanced to Charlotte, then to Theo. Her eyes went wide. "Hi, doggy!"

Dennis chuckled. "That's Theo, and the nice lady holding his leash is Miss Charlotte."

His daughter smiled at Charlotte. "Nice to meet you. Can I pet your dog?"

Panic flashed across Charlotte's face. She swallowed and regained her composure. "Likewise, Amelia. And yes, Theo loves head scratches."

Amelia rushed to Theo and oohed and aahed over him, but Dennis noticed Charlotte taking a step back. Did the woman have a problem with his daughter? Or was his overprotectiveness taking over? Charlotte had gone through a harrowing experience last night. Maybe she was overwhelmed. That's all. He brushed off the odd reaction.

"I…um… Could I leave Theo here while I get cleaned up? If I put him *on place*, he'll stay until I get back." Charlotte grabbed her bag, her eyes wide and full of distress.

"Sure. Not a problem." What had spooked her?

She dug into her backpack, removed the same wool blanket he'd used only hours ago and placed it on the ground by the fireplace.

"Hold on. Let me get him something dry." Dennis sifted through the basket under the window. "Here." He folded and laid a thick blanket on the floor.

"Thank you." She pointed to the makeshift bed. "Theo, *place*." Theo trotted over and plopped down with a huff.

Amelia giggled at the dog's frustration.

"Down the hall, first door on your right. The bedroom has an en suite bathroom. Make yourself at home. Grab a nap if you'd like."

"Thanks, but a shower will be fine." She hefted her go-bag onto her shoulder, strode to his guest room and disappeared through the doorway.

What had gotten into her? And why did Amelia's presence seem to send her mentally running for the hills?

"Come on, Daddy. I'll fix you breakfast." Amelia slid her tiny hand into his.

The statement shredded his heart. No five-year-old should ever think they had to be a caregiver.

Amy, who stood by the kitchen archway, tossed the towel she'd held onto her shoulder. "Tell you what, kiddo, why don't I fix a plate for your dad while you tell him about your slumber party with your aunts and uncles?"

Amelia tugged him to the table. "Uncle Jason made popcorn, and we watched *Frozen*." She held her hands to her chest and spun. "Oh, Daddy, it was so much fun."

While his daughter continued to chatter on about her night, Amy handed him a cup of coffee. "You look like you could use this."

"You have no idea. Thank you." He sipped the hot liquid and let it warm his insides. "So I take it you had fun?"

"I did." Amelia took her plate to the sink, rinsed it and put it in the dishwasher. Another sign of the adult things she'd had to do when her mother left her home alone or came back too high on drugs to function. "Daddy, I love you, but can I go to school now? Mrs. Peterson said we're painting today, and I don't want to miss it."

"You sure can, sweetheart." He turned to Amy. "Would you mind taking her? I'd like to see if a little hot water will chase away the chill."

"Of course. Come on, Amelia. Let's get you to school."

His daughter kissed him on the cheek. "Bye, Daddy."

He watched her skip to her bedroom to get her backpack. "Thank you, Amy. I can't tell you how much I appreciate all you've done."

"I have an idea." She smiled. "Go get warm."

"Yes, ma'am." He threw back the remainder of his coffee and headed to his bedroom for a long-awaited shower.

On the way, he glanced at Charlotte's closed door. He'd vowed to himself that he'd keep her safe, but what was up with the fact she could barely look at his daughter?

Charlotte stepped from the bathroom, her wet hair hanging limp on her shoulders. Her jeans and sweatshirt felt wonderful on her warm skin, and her wool socks cocooned her cold feet. Between the hot shower and dry clothes, the chill from last night had finally faded. She towel-dried her hair, then twisted it and secured it with a clip.

After stuffing her belongings into her duffel, she eased the door open and meandered to the living room, where she found a snoring Theo. The scent of fresh coffee drifted from the kitchen. She'd let Theo rest. He deserved it after working hard yesterday. She padded into the kitchen and found a clean mug that Amy must have left for her. She poured herself a cup and held the steaming liquid under her chin. The bold aroma tantalized her senses.

She inhaled the scent and took a sip. Warmth flooded her veins and finished chasing away the remaining chill.

The back door flew open, and Amelia ran into the kitchen. "Forgot my book."

Charlotte jostled her cup and dropped it to the floor. Brown liquid pooled beneath her feet, soaking her socks.

Amelia came to an abrupt stop at the table. "I'm sorry. I didn't mean to scare you. I can clean it up."

"It's okay. I'm fine." Her words sounded stiff even to her. "Go ahead. You don't want to be late."

Amelia nodded, grabbed her book from the table and disappeared out the door.

Tears burned behind Charlotte's eyes. She released the breath she'd held when she stared at the five-year-old. Coming to Dennis's house was a mistake.

She loved children, however five-year-old girls gave her pause. But this time of year—the week of her baby's birthday—was different. The grief pulled her under and tore her heart to shreds, emphasizing her loss in neon lights. She'd yet to figure out how to move past the hole in her life.

Dennis skidded around the corner of the kitchen doorway with Theo on his heels. "What happened?"

She stared at his dripping hair and the damp clothes that clung to his skin, trying to make sense of his worry. She glanced to the floor. "Oh, I dropped my coffee mug."

He placed his hand over his chest. "From behind a closed door, it sounded like a gunshot. I was too far away to help."

Theo took a step toward her. "Theo, *stay*." The dog whined but obeyed. "Amelia came running in. She forgot her book. It startled me, and I dropped the cup."

His gaze shifted to the floor. Charlotte saw exactly when the mess registered in his brain. "Don't move. Let me get something to clean up the mess."

She stood motionless while he threw the pieces away and mopped up the coffee.

"There. All done. But I think you'll need another pair of socks. Have a seat at the table, and I'll get you some." Dennis returned a minute later and handed her a wet washcloth and replacement socks.

"Thank you." She cleaned her feet and slipped on the socks, then moved to the living room and tossed the wet ones in her bag with the rest of her dirty clothes. "Sorry about that. I hope the cup wasn't a keepsake."

"No. It was a dollar-store special, so no worries. Let's try again. You look like you could use that cup of coffee."

Charlotte rubbed her arms and followed Dennis into the kitchen. She lowered herself onto a chair. Theo tagged along and lay across her feet. "Coffee sounds amazing. The chill from last night really settled in my bones."

Dennis retrieved his mug from the sink and a new one from the cupboard and poured coffee into them. He set the cream and sugar on the table, then placed the cup in front of her. "There. Drink up." He took a sip and leveled his gaze on her. "I thought with your job, you'd be more comfortable around kids, but I guess not."

She lifted the mug to her lips and froze. "What do you mean?"

He shrugged. "Just that you're all stiff around my daughter. I know she can be a whirlwind, but…"

How did she explain? Telling him the real reason would expose wounds she had no intention of ever opening again. That's why she never planned to have children. The pain from the memories were too great.

"Charlotte?"

She blinked and realized she'd spaced out. She shook her head. "I like children. That's why I work with expectant mothers."

"So is it just my daughter?"

The hole she dug got deeper. "No, it's not that."

"Then what's wrong?"

"She reminds me of a little girl that died." There. It was the truth. Not all of it, but enough.

"I'm sorry. I didn't mean to pry." He ran a hand over his face. "I'm protective of Amelia."

"And for good reason."

He nodded. "But I shouldn't have made a snap judgment about you. It's not normally my style."

From what she'd heard, the man had a gentle personality, but stress did funny things to people. And their situation was nothing if not stressful. "I'll tell you what, let's put it aside and figure out our next step in finding Hannah and why someone is shooting at us. Hannah's still missing, and I'm worried. It's not like her."

He studied her for a moment and gave a quick nod. "My deputies are on the shooter. They'll keep us updated. I want us focused on Hannah. You told me about her and her boyfriend. Are you sure he had nothing to do with her disappearance?"

"I can't see it. They really do love each other. They're young and not ready for a baby, but Hannah talked about the possibility of changing her mind. If she told him, I don't know how he'd react to that."

Dennis took a drink and set the mug on the table, cupping it in both hands. "Maybe he didn't like it and got angry, and Hannah ran from him. It wouldn't be the first time something like that happened."

Charlotte considered the possibility but rejected it. "I still say no."

"Why don't we go find the young man and ask him a few questions?" Dennis stood, gathered their mugs and put them in the sink. He gestured toward Theo, who'd fallen asleep over her feet. "I have a covered back patio and a fenced-in backyard if you'd like to leave him here. I could make him a warm bed if you want."

She reached down and ran her fingers through the dog's fur. As much as she wanted Theo with her, he deserved a lazy day. "I think he'd like that."

"I'll go set things up for him and finish getting ready."

Dennis left to make a comfortable place for her dog. The man was a nice guy. Considerate. And, for all intents and purposes, easygoing. She couldn't deny being drawn to him, but he had a daughter the same age as her baby would have been. She couldn't ignore that, nor could she handle the constant nearness to Amelia.

FIVE

Thursday 10:00 a.m.

Careful of the snow-covered ice patches on the streets, Dennis took care maneuvering through town and made his way toward the grocery store where Jordan Miller worked. A quick call to the store manager had confirmed the kid was there and on shift for another few hours.

"Do you think he'll willingly talk to us?" Dennis had never met the young man, which was odd for such a small town. Although, he shopped at a different grocery store, and since Jordan hadn't caused trouble, it explained not knowing the teen.

"I don't see why not. We only want to find Hannah." Charlotte stared out the passenger window. "I hope he has information that will help us."

Dennis pulled into the parking lot and killed the engine. He still wasn't comfortable having Charlotte out in the open after yesterday. Someone had wanted her dead, and Dennis had no illusion that the bad guy would walk away without finishing the job. "Please, stay close to me. I don't like the fact my deputies haven't found the person who shot at us."

She leaned against her door and turned her attention to him. "You really know how to boost a girl's confidence."

"Just the truth. I want you aware of your surroundings."

She opened her door, slid out and spun to face him before closing it. "Noted. And, Dennis, I'm not careless or a pushover."

No, she wasn't. The woman had proved she had the ability to think on her feet. "Glad to hear it." He exited the driver's side, smiling at her spunk. He walked around the front of the vehicle and placed his hand on the small of her lower back. "Let's go find Jordan."

They made it halfway to the entrance of the store when Charlotte spotted the teen. "There. In the blue shirt."

He scanned the section of the parking lot she'd indicated. "I see him." Dennis veered toward the young man.

When Jordan saw them, he took off running toward the park down the street.

"Jordan! Stop!" Dennis sprinted after him. His boots pounded on the ground, and he heard Charlotte's footfalls not far behind, confirming she'd followed him.

The kid hit the park and wove through the benches surrounding the play structure. He dodged the trees dotting the perimeter of the grassy area, heading to the woods that lay beyond.

Dennis put on a burst of speed and tackled him to the snowy ground. He clamped his hand onto Jordan's arm. "Stop fighting. I only want to talk to you." He flipped the kid over and sucked in a breath at the sudden movement. Not only was his body screaming at him after last night's adventure, but he was once again covered in snow.

Charlotte caught up with them and placed her hands on her knees while she caught her breath.

Dennis helped Jordan to his feet but kept a firm grasp on the kid's forearm so that he didn't run again.

The young man cringed and tucked his chin to his chest. "Please, don't hit me. I don't know anything."

"Relax. I'm Sheriff Dennis Monroe. I'm not going to hurt you." Dennis loosened his grip but kept hold of the kid.

Jordan looked up. Bruises marred his face, and uncertainty lined his features. "You're really the sheriff?"

What happened to scare this kid? And who had hurt him? Dennis nodded. "How'd you get the black eye and fat lip?"

"Some guy cornered me and wanted to know where Hannah was. He didn't like my answer."

"And what answer was that?"

"That she'd taken off, and I had no clue where she went. Then he started pounding on me. But you can't tell what you don't know." Jordan shrugged and averted his eyes.

Dennis studied the kid. The young man knew more than he let on. But how much more was the real question.

Charlotte stepped closer and placed a hand on Jordan's shoulder. "I'm really worried about Hannah and the baby. I know you love her, Jordan. Anything you can tell us that might help would be great."

The kid looked down at Dennis's hand and back up to him. Dennis let go but stayed close in case Jordan decided to bolt.

"Jordan, I think you're a brave young man who is trying to protect the woman he loves." He folded his arms across his chest. "But I also think you know more than you're telling us."

Jordan rubbed the back of his neck and scanned the area. Tension flowed off him as he appeared to ponder what to say. He looked at

Charlotte and jerked his head toward Dennis. "Is he really okay, Miss B?"

Charlotte chuckled.

Dennis raised a brow, curious at the kid's nickname for Charlotte and his question. He and Charlotte had survived being shot at and almost freezing to death in a makeshift cave. He wondered if that had earned her trust or if he was doomed to continue to prove himself to her.

She eyed him up and down as if trying to decide, then smiled. "He's one of the good guys. I promise."

Dennis released the breath he hadn't realized he'd held while waiting on her response. Why had it mattered so much to him? But he didn't have time to ponder the question. He had a job to do. He returned his focus to the teen.

Jordan didn't look so sure about Charlotte's assessment but nodded. "Okay, if you're sure. Hannah came to me in tears a couple days ago. Said she'd changed her mind and wanted to keep our baby."

"And how did you respond?" Charlotte asked.

"I… We got into an argument." Jordan dipped his head. "I don't know anything about raising a baby. And how am I going to provide for a family? I work part-time at a grocery store." He threw his hands in the air.

"So you argued. Hannah got scared and ran

away." The girl's actions made sense if the kid had lost his temper, but it didn't solve who'd shot at Charlotte or killed Stella.

"No, sir." The young man shook his head. "I admit, it took me a while to settle down, but we talked it out."

"And what did you decide?" Charlotte's calm tone amazed him. She had a way of easing people's worry. A charming quality he found fascinating.

"She'd made up her mind about the baby, but we agreed to take a little time to think about what that would look like."

"Meaning?" Dennis asked.

"Meaning, whether or not we should get married or if she should live with her parents while we continue to date. You know, make sure we were getting married for the right reasons, not just because of the baby."

The kid's maturity shocked Dennis. Would he have done the same if Tina had given him the chance? He hoped so, but he honestly wasn't sure how he would've responded. When he'd first found out Tina was pregnant, he'd made the decision to marry her, but she panicked and took off.

Little had he known that Tina had already moved on to another guy. The next time they saw each other, she told him she'd miscarried the baby. Only she hadn't. If he'd taken the time to really think things over, maybe his daughter wouldn't have suffered, and he wouldn't have missed five years of her life.

"Sounds reasonable. Were her parents agreeable?" Charlotte asked.

Dennis pulled his thoughts from the past and refocused.

"I think so. She said they were." Jordan toed a hole in the snow.

Charlotte placed a hand on the teen's arm. "What did she do after your conversation?"

"She said she was going home."

"She never made it." Dennis studied the teen. Jordan appeared to be telling the truth. "Who else did she tell about keeping the baby?"

Jordan shrugged. "I assume her parents, since she said they'd help. Oh, and she told Erin."

Not knowing who Erin was, Dennis looked at Charlotte.

"Her social worker, Erin Rivers." Charlotte turned her attention back to Jordan. "Anyone else?"

The kid shook his head. "I don't think so. She might have told her friends Stella and Ginny, but I have no idea."

Charlotte's gaze flickered to Dennis.

He shook his head, not ready to tell Jordan what had happened to Stella. If the teen was on the up and up, which Dennis thought he was, he didn't want to scare the kid.

Dennis changed the direction of the conversation. "Hannah had no reason that you know of to run away. So let's back up and talk about the guy who assaulted you."

Jordan's eyes widened. "What about him?"

"Do you know him?"

"I have no idea who he is. I've never seen him before in my life." Jordan's breathing rate increased, and his voice rose.

Dennis held his palms out. "Calm down. It's okay. Can you describe him?"

Jordan ran a hand over his head. "He's a little over six foot. Slightly taller than me. Kinda rough looking, like he's done a lot of drugs."

"That's good. What color is his hair? His eyes?"

"Brown hair, but I never noticed the color of his eyes."

"Anything else that can help us ID him?"

"Like what?"

"Say a tattoo or scar? A birthmark, maybe?"

The crease between Jordan's eyes deepened. "He had a scar along his jaw, I think."

"Is that all?"

The kid nodded.

Dennis gripped his shoulder. "You did good, Jordan. I'll let my deputies know to look out for him. I just wish you'd reported this when it happened."

"I was scared. He told me to keep my mouth shut, so I did." Jordan touched his eye. "Didn't want to go through that again."

"I get it. I really do." Dennis understood the teen's reluctance. He'd taken a beating and probably feared for his life and Hannah's.

"I'm proud of you, Jordan." Charlotte gave the young man a quick hug. "Hang in there. If anyone can find this guy, it's Sheriff Monroe."

The woman had a lot of confidence in Dennis, and he didn't want to disappoint her. "We appreciate the information." He removed a business card from his wallet and held it out to Jordan. "If you can think of anything else, please let me know."

Jordan stared at the card as if it might bite him.

"I'm here to help. Really." Dennis prayed the young man took the card.

"Jordan, I know you're scared and confused with everything going on. We just want to find Hannah and make sure she's okay." Charlotte took the card, placed it in Jordan's hand, then wrapped his fingers around it. "Please."

The young man's shoulders lifted and fell. He nodded.

"Thank you." Charlotte rubbed a hand down his arm.

"I should get back to work before I don't have a job."

"Sounds like a good idea." Dennis pointed to the business card. "Feel free to call about anything. Even if you just need to talk."

A smile curved Jordan's lips. "Thanks." The kid stuffed his hands in his pockets and hurried toward the grocery store.

"At least we now know something about Hannah's last movements." Charlotte adjusted the zipper on her coat. "What do you think?"

"I think that young man is confused and overwhelmed, but my gut says he didn't hurt his girlfriend. He might know more than he's telling us, but I'm not sure. He certainly didn't know about Stella."

"I agree. Let's see if we can talk with Ginny. Maybe she knows where Hannah is."

Dennis motioned for Charlotte to head toward the truck. They caught up with Jordan, who'd stopped at the curb, waiting for several cars to pass.

The hair stood on the back of Dennis's neck. His hand shot to his holster and hovered over his weapon.

Charlotte turned to face him. "Dennis?"

He could feel Charlotte and Jordan watching him, but he kept his focus on the surrounding area, searching for whatever had caused his reaction.

"I don't like—"

Gunshots cracked in the air.

Jordan cried out and crumpled to the ground.

Dennis tackled Charlotte and yanked the Glock from his holster.

People screamed in the background, but Jordan and Charlotte were his main concern. He looked down at the woman he'd taken to the ground. "Are you okay?"

She grimaced but nodded. "Go. Help Jordan."

He hated leaving her unprotected, but the blood pooling under the young man worried him. Dennis crawled to the kid. "Jordan. Can you hear me?" He rolled him over to get a better look at the wound and blew out a long breath. The bullet had hit Jordan in the shoulder. Painful, yes, but not life-threatening, as long as medical help got there quick. "Charlotte, we need to get out of here."

She moved next to him. "You grab him under his arms, and I'll get his legs."

Dennis wasn't sure how he'd move the kid without causing extreme pain, but that was better than leaving him in the open to get shot again. He hooked his arms under Jordan's and met Charlotte's eyes. "Ready?"

She nodded.

"On three, we head behind that silver car." He tightened his grip. "One, two, three."

He lifted and cringed when a guttural moan escaped Jordan. "Sorry, dude." They ducked behind the car and lowered Jordan to the ground. Dennis took off his jacket, yanked off the button-up shirt he wore over an undershirt and pressed it to the kid's bleeding shoulder. Sirens whined in the distance. "Hang in there. Help is coming."

For the first time since the gunshots, Dennis allowed his gaze to roam over Charlotte, checking for injuries. Rips and splotches of blood stood out on the knees of her pants, and a red mark on her cheek had started to swell and turn purple. His chest tightened. He'd done that to her when he'd tackled her.

"I'm sorry, Charlotte."

"For what?" Her brows pinched together.

He jutted his chin toward her legs. "I hurt you."

"Sheriff Monroe." She placed her hands on her hips and scowled.

Uh-oh, the formality was almost as bad as a parent using a child's full name.

"You protected me. I'm alive. I'm not going to complain about minor scrapes."

Minor? He cringed. "I think it's a little more than a simple scratch."

"Dennis." She softened her tone. "I admit, it

stings, but I'll be fine. Please, don't blame yourself for doing your job."

The woman continued to amaze him. She'd taken the snowstorm in stride and kept her wits about her. Her quick thinking had saved his life. Now, she appeared unaffected by a gunman and the injuries marring her face and knees. She had more grit than he'd originally given her credit for. If only she liked his daughter, he might be interested in getting to know her better, but loving Amelia was nonnegotiable.

Blue and red lights flashed and sirens whined. Patrol cars arrived in quick succession followed by an ambulance.

Charlotte placed her hands over Dennis's and pressed against Jordan's shoulder. "I've got this. Go talk to the officers."

He studied her a moment, then transferred Jordan's care to her and hurried off.

"Hey, Jordan. How are you doing?" She smiled, hoping that even though she couldn't relieve his pain, she might be able to ease his worry.

"Been better, Miss B."

Charlotte chuckled. "I see you've picked up on Hannah's nickname for me."

He nodded and grimaced. "She really likes you."

"I like her too. Very much." She glanced over

her shoulder. What was taking the paramedics so long?

"I'm scared, Miss B. For myself and Hannah. This guy isn't letting up. I don't understand what he wants. Please find her before he hurts her." Jordan gasped out each word.

"Easy now. Try to relax." She continued the pressure and leaned in. "Sheriff Monroe will do his best. We won't stop until we figure out what happened and bring her home."

His hand clutched hers. "Thank you."

She nodded. "You are very welcome."

"Hey there, my man, what's your name?" A paramedic dropped beside her, slipped his hand beneath hers and whispered, "I've got him."

Charlotte eased away, giving the paramedic full access to the teen.

"Jordan."

"Nice to meet you, Jordan. I'm Brent, and that ugly mug on the other side of you is Ethan. We're going to get you hooked up to an IV and give you something for the pain. Then we'll get you out of here and to the hospital so the doctors can fuss over you."

Ethan expertly slid the needle into Jordan's arm and set up the IV.

"Sounds good." Jordan's words slurred. "Miss B."

She peered over Brent's shoulder. "I'm here."

His eyes fluttered open. "When you find her, tell her I'm all in."

Charlotte forced a smile. "You can tell her yourself."

Jordan struggled to sit up, and Ethan eased him down.

"Please. She needs to know."

"I will, Jordan. I promise."

"Good, good." He closed his eyes.

Charlotte folded her arms and crossed her wrists in front of her palms up, careful not to get blood on her clothes, while Brent and Ethan packed Jordan's wound and moved him to the gurney.

"Charlotte." Dennis closed the distance. "Are you okay?"

"Just worried about him." She pointed to Jordan as the paramedics loaded him into the ambulance.

"He's in good hands. Brent and Ethan are the best." Dennis held out a water bottle. "Here. Let's take care of that blood."

She glanced at her hands and nodded.

"Hold them out in front of you." She obliged, and he poured the water over them as she rubbed them together. "Officer Davis with Valley Springs PD thought you might like to clean up."

"That was nice of him." Pink water flowed from her fingertips. Jordan had lost a lot of blood, but his prognosis was positive. She prayed that complications wouldn't arise to change the outcome. Hannah and the baby needed him. The bottle empty, Charlotte shook her hands and wiped them on her pants. "Thank you."

Dennis cupped her chin and tilted her face upward. "That's a serious scrape and bruise on your cheek on top of the one from yesterday." He stepped back, ran his gaze from her head to her feet and frowned.

She glanced down at her ripped jeans and bloodied knees. Not until that moment had she noticed the cuts. Now the torn skin burned like a thousand bee stings. Her cheek throbbed in time with her heart, and the road rash on her palms didn't feel any better.

He motioned to all her injuries and cringed. "Did I do all that?"

She hated to admit it, but his actions had caused her injuries. "I'll take this over dead any day." Charlotte rolled her aching neck, then smirked. "Let me guess, you played linebacker in high school."

"Ha ha, very funny." The corner of his mouth curved upward. "Actually, it was right tackle, and it was in college."

She blinked and burst out laughing.

Dennis shrugged. "Well, it's true."

It felt good to find some levity in all this craziness. She stilled as the memory of the gunshot. Jordan's pale face replayed in her mind. "Do you think he's gone?"

"The shooter?"

She nodded. She hadn't missed Dennis's scan of the area. It was almost imperceptible, but it was there. His relaxed stance gave away none of his concerns.

"Valley Springs PD is doing a search, but I'm guessing the shooter took off when he heard the sirens."

"Do you think Jordan was his target, or was the shooter after me?" Charlotte rubbed at the raw skin on the heel of her hand.

He wrapped his fingers around her wrist. "Stop. You'll only make it worse. Why don't we swing by the hospital and get you checked out before we head home?"

Charlotte shook her head. "I don't need a doctor. Just a little soap and water, and maybe some ointment to put on the scrapes."

"Are you sure?"

"Positive." Add to that list several ibuprofens and she might feel human again. "I'd like to go by my office at Sadie's Place first, if that's okay."

"Sure. But may I ask what for?"

"I have an extra set of clothes there, and it's quicker than the thirty-minute drive home. Plus,

I'd like to grab my laptop with my notes on the girls. I feel like I'm missing something."

"No problem. We'll head to Sadie's Place, then to my house afterward. I'll let Officer Davis know where to find us if he has any more questions." He cupped her elbow and led her to his truck.

She climbed in, careful not to bend her knees too much and irritate her wounds. He closed the door with a soft snick and jogged to the patrol officer standing off to the side.

After a quick chat, Dennis hurried back and slipped into the truck. "Ready?"

"Sure."

He pulled from the parking lot. "I called my deputy Kyle, and he's going to pick up Amelia for me and drop her off at the house since I won't make it to the school in time. We can go over what we know while I wait on Amy to pick up the princess for the remainder of the day."

"Your daughter's going to be there?" Charlotte wanted to grab her dog and SUV and escape the grief pressing down on her, but Hannah was still missing, and now Jordan had a bullet in his shoulder. Not to mention poor Stella and her missing baby. No. Charlotte had to suck it up and try to keep the memories from invading. It wasn't Amelia's fault she was the same age as Charlotte's baby girl would've been if she'd lived.

Why couldn't she let it go? Five years had passed. Surely, by now, she should have moved on? But grief was a funny thing. It hung on in the weirdest places and showed itself at the strangest times. If only they'd let her hold her baby and given her closure.

Dennis glanced at her, then returned his focus to the road. "Is there a problem with that?"

"No." She swallowed the lie. No desire to explain, she stayed quiet and watched the trees along the side of the street whiz by.

SIX

Thursday 11:30 a.m.

The one thing Dennis hated was lying. And Charlotte had told a whopper. He knew the woman had an issue with Amelia. She held something back, and he wanted to know what.

He pulled into the parking lot of Sadie's Place and cut the engine. Charlotte stared out the passenger window, off in another world. She hadn't realized they'd arrived. He patted her arm. "Ready?"

She startled and whipped her attention to him. "Sorry. I guess I zoned out there for a moment."

"No biggie. I'm sure you have a lot on your mind." He pulled the keys from the ignition. "Shall we go in?"

"Sure." She got out, closed the door and strode to the entrance without another word.

He held the door open, and she limped inside. His frustration from his perception of her feelings toward his daughter cooled a bit, knowing he was responsible for Charlotte's latest injuries. Yes, he'd protected her, but he still felt horrible for causing her pain. Maybe his oversensitivity had caused him to misunderstand her hesitation and her response had nothing to do with Amelia.

"This way." She led him down the hallway on the right to a set of rooms, opened her office door and flipped on the light. "Come on in. Give me a few minutes to gather my things."

"Go ahead. Do what you need to do." Dennis ambled in and took note of the tidy surfaces and comfortable chairs in the corner. The light green wall mixed with floral pictures gave the space a calming effect. One he envisioned her clients appreciating. He strolled around the medium-size office and studied her credentials hanging on the wall. A smile curved on his lips when he noticed the dog bed next to her desk. "Does Theo come to work with you often?"

Charlotte halted her movement and noticed what had triggered his question. "He's been known to help me with my counseling sessions from time to time." She grinned.

"I have a feeling he's good at it."

"Without a doubt." She turned back to her task and tucked some clothes into a plastic bag and grabbed her laptop. After a quick glance around the room, she faced him. "I think I have everything."

Voices rose in the office across the hall.

Dennis poked his head out and read the nameplate next to the door. *Erin Rivers, LCSW.* "Does your social worker always have heated conversations?"

"Not normally." Arms full, she peeked around him. "Oh, my. Whatever's going on, she's not happy."

They stood listening to the argument until curiosity got the best of him. "Who's she yelling at?"

Charlotte leaned her ear toward Erin's door. "Sounds like Troy Kent, the attorney we work with."

"Should we be worried?" He'd seen one too many arguments turn violent not to be concerned.

"I don't think so. Even though this is out of character, neither are the type to come to blows over a disagreement."

The shouting match ended and the voices lowered, easing his worry. "Wonder what got her so riled up?"

"Who knows, but let's get out of here. I don't want to get caught eavesdropping."

He chuckled. "Do you have everything?"

"Yes." She pushed him out the door and locked it behind her. "Keep walking."

Dennis hustled down the hall until they were out of earshot. "Better?"

She glared at him. "You think you're funny, don't you?"

"No. But I find it interesting that you're worried about overhearing a shouting match."

"Am not. I… Well…okay, so I feel guilty about eavesdropping. Satisfied?" A smirk grew on her lips.

He enjoyed seeing another side to her. One that intrigued him, but he couldn't forget her aversion to Amelia. "Let's go." His clipped words surprised even him.

She blinked then hurried to his SUV. When he clicked the key fob and unlocked the doors, she climbed in.

He blew out a long breath. He'd messed up again. The poor woman must have whiplash from his constant change in attitude. He slid into the driver's seat and headed home.

It was lunchtime, and Charlotte still sported her injuries from the shooting. Food and a first-aid kit were on the top of the to-do list.

After he parked the vehicle, he escorted her into the house and hung up their jackets.

"Let's get you cleaned up." Dennis cupped her elbow and guided her to the couch. "Have a seat. I'll get the first-aid kit and take care of those scrapes. Then I'll fix us some lunch." Charlotte complied, and he headed to the kitchen.

A black nose pressed against the door to the back patio. Dennis grinned. Someone wanted to see his owner. He opened the door, expecting the English shepherd to dart in, but Theo sat and tilted his head, waiting for an invitation.

"I have a feeling your mom could use you right now. Come on in, Theo." Dennis stepped aside, and the dog hurried past.

"Theo!" Charlotte's voice carried from the other room.

He grabbed a wet washcloth and the first-aid kit and followed in the dog's wake.

Theo soaked up the hug and scratches from his owner. The dog's tongue hung out off to the side, and his eyes practically rolled to the back of his head. Charlotte's facial features softened now that Theo had joined her.

"Here we go." He sat next to her on the couch, wiped her hands, arms and knees with the cloth, then opened the kit. "Let me get ointment on these and put some bandages on the wounds."

"Thank you." Charlotte brushed the back of her hand over Theo's head.

He felt like a heel for snapping at her. "Listen, I'm sorry for the mood swing back at your office."

She sucked in a quick breath when he dabbed

the cuts on her knee. "Want to tell me what it was about?"

He sighed. "Amelia."

"And whether or not I like her?"

Not trusting himself to speak, he nodded.

Charlotte bit her lower lip. "It's not that I—"

"Daddy!" Amelia ran in, jumped into his lap and threw her arms around his neck.

The force of her exuberance slammed him against the back of the couch. He tossed the first-aid supplies onto the coffee table and wrapped Amelia in a hug. "Hey there, princess. How was school?"

"It was great! Mrs. Peterson loved my painting. I can't wait until I can bring it home." Amelia's eyes widened when she noticed Charlotte and Theo. "Hi, Miss Charlotte. Hi, doggy."

"Hello, Amelia." A strained smile pulled on Charlotte's lips. "Would you like to pet Theo?"

His daughter's head bobbed. "Yes, please." She climbed down and knelt next to the dog.

"He loves to be scratched behind the ears."

Theo practically groaned with pleasure at the girl's attention.

"Amelia, if you'll take care of Theo for me, I'll go change my ripped jeans."

"Sure. Theo and I are best friends." His little girl snuggled into the dog's neck. "Aren't we, boy?"

Charlotte grabbed her duffel from where she'd left it earlier, plus her bag of clothes from the office and ambled to the extra bedroom.

At least she'd attempted to be more cordial to his daughter.

"Hey, boss." Kyle waltzed in. "That girl is fast. She made it inside before I even got out of the car."

Dennis chuckled. "Welcome to my world."

His deputy collapsed onto the recliner. "What can I do to help?"

"You already have."

Kyle stayed quiet and waited him out.

Dennis crossed his ankle over his knee and toyed with the hem of his pants. "I need to fix some lunch, then I'd like to go over what we have and see if we can connect the dots."

"Doug is staying in the loop with Valley Springs PD since they have jurisdiction of the shooting."

"Good. Your partner's excellent at working with VSPD." Dennis relaxed, knowing they'd have access to the evidence.

Kyle jutted his chin toward the hallway. "I heard the details about what happened. How's she doing?"

"She's tough. I don't think it'll stop her from searching for Hannah."

"Good." Kyle drew in a deep breath. "How are *you* doing, Dennis?"

Ah, the code for a change from boss to friend. "I'm okay. I don't think it's sunk in yet. I haven't let my mind go there." If one of the bullets had hit him, Amelia would be an orphan. The thought jolted him. *Thank You, God, for not letting that happen.*

He'd added a quick addendum to his will when he took custody of Amelia, but after today, he'd better get it completely in order and name a legal guardian for his daughter in case the unthinkable happened. As a law enforcement officer, he faced the possibility of losing his life on the job. He had training, and the best deputies out there had his back, but reality had him making a mental note to call his attorney once he wasn't trying to find Hannah or track down a killer.

"We're all here for you. You know that, right?"

Dennis rubbed the back of his neck. "Yeah. And I couldn't have made it this far without all of you."

Amelia stood and pointed to the dog bed. "Theo, *place*." She skipped over to Dennis. "Would you and Uncle Kyle like some lunch? I can make it."

The grown-up words sliced his heart. "Honey, you don't have to do that. In fact, why don't I go make something for everyone?"

Her smile drooped. "Okay, Daddy."

The change in Amelia's demeanor worried him. He'd run into, for lack of better terms, triggers since the day Amelia arrived on his doorstep. And something he'd said a minute ago had hit the unwanted mark. He and Kyle exchanged looks. Neither knew the cause for her switch in mood.

Whatever the reason, he planned to keep catering to his daughter's needs. Dennis had tried since she'd come to live with him, but Amelia had lived her short life as a caregiver to her drug-addict mother and insisted on taking care of him. If only he'd known about Amelia, but he couldn't turn back the clock.

"It'll only take me a few minutes, princess."

Amelia shrugged, then laid next to Theo and ran her hand over the dog's fur.

Kyle grabbed a magazine from the coffee table and started flipping pages. "Holler if you need anything."

Dennis waved a hand and proceeded to the kitchen, thankful his friend intended to keep an eye on Amelia.

A few minutes later, he had sandwiches and chips plated, along with a juice box and three coffees ready. He grabbed his daughter's lunch first.

"Can I help with anything?"

He spun and came eye to eye with Charlotte.

"Oh, hi. Yes, please. If you can give me a hand with the coffees, that would be great."

"Sure." She grabbed all three mugs and took them into the living room like a pro.

He placed Amelia's food and drink on the coffee table. "Lunch is ready, sweetie."

"Coming, Daddy." His heart settled hearing the lilt in Amelia's voice return. She moved to the low table and plopped down.

Dennis took the cup that Charlotte offered. "Let me guess. You waitressed your way through college."

"No." Her smile faded. "It's how I survived in high school."

Another layer to Charlotte he knew nothing about yet wanted to peel back.

The group ate the simple meal while listening to Amelia's monologue about her day. When she finished, she gathered everyone's plates and took them to the kitchen. "I'll put these in the sink and go do my homework."

A protest sat on Dennis's lips, but he refrained. "Thanks, sweetie."

Charlotte eyed him. "What kind of homework does a kindergartener have?"

"Her teacher works with the second-grade teacher to give Amelia something to challenge her." He watched his daughter skip to her room. "I have a feeling Mrs. Peterson is going to have to up her game. She's already bored with the second-grade work."

"Wow."

"No kidding. I was a solid B student. I'm out of my league with her. She'll be doing calculus before she turns ten at this point."

Kyle laughed. "Glad it's you and not me. I barely passed algebra."

"Trust me, I know. I've seen you do math," Dennis teased. He brushed his hands together to clean off the chip crumbs and rested back against the couch cushions. "If y'all are ready, I'd like to go over everything that's happened." He turned to Charlotte. "Now that we've talked to Jordan, I'd like you to dig through your memory and see if you can come up with any new ideas as to where Hannah might hide."

Charlotte bit her bottom lip, thought for a moment, then shook her head.

Kyle leaned forward and rested his elbows on his knees. "Anything would help."

She exhaled. "I honestly don't know. But I'm worried. Hannah's missing, and Stella is dead. Why? And where's the baby?"

"Jason and Keith are driving Melanie crazy, bugging her about the autopsy. They're on Stella's case and will keep us up to date with any information they discover," Kyle said.

The whole situation didn't add up. "So other

than Hannah and Stella sharing the fact they were pregnant, are there any other connections?"

Charlotte's brow furrowed, and she stared at a spot on the wall. "Not that I can think of. Hannah's parents are supportive. Plus, she has Jordan. Stella is—was—alone in the world. Her parents disowned her, and I have no idea who the baby's father is."

"Well, there has to be something." The shooting earlier that day played on his mind. He stilled. Could Charlotte be the connection? "Until now, I thought the shooter was after Jordan, but that second shot was aimed at you."

She stiffened. "What are you talking about? There was only one shot, and that hit Jordan."

"Charlotte, the gunman fired twice. The first one hit the kid. The second missed you and hit the ground about a foot from your head."

"Two?" Her chin quivered.

He nodded. He hadn't realized she'd thought the gunman had only fired once. "I'm worried that you're a part of this."

A single tear rolled down her cheek. "But why?"

"If we knew that, we'd be closer to having the person in custody," Kyle joined in. "I promise that we won't stop until we have answers."

"He's right. My deputies are the best around. Not to mention stubborn. They'll get to the bottom of this." His detectives had come through for each other and for him when Amelia arrived unannounced in his life. Dennis glanced at his daughter, who'd returned to the living room and now sat next to Theo, reading him a story. The dog actually looked interested. Maybe getting a dog would help Amelia settle into having a normal childhood. His thoughts whirled back to the moment he'd realized the shooter had aimed at Charlotte. He returned his attention to her. "I think you need to be alert—"

Charlotte's phone rang. She glanced at the caller ID and tensed. "I'm sorry, I need to take this." She stood and walked to the entry for privacy.

The more Dennis pondered the events over the last twenty-four hours, the more convinced he'd become that Charlotte was in danger.

Phone to her ear, Charlotte paced the small entry. "Ginny, what's wrong?" The panic in the girl's voice worried her.

"Please, Miss B, I have to see you." Ginny's sobs intensified.

She glanced in Dennis's direction. He'd accompanied her everywhere so far, but his daughter needed him. Charlotte rubbed her forehead. It might not be smart with a killer on the loose, but with or without him, she'd go anywhere for one of her girls. "Tell me where, and I'll be there."

"Thank you." Ginny sniffed. "Meet me at Henry's Gas Station."

"All right. I'll be there as soon as I can." She hated to take Dennis away from Amelia, but there was no way he'd let her go alone, so she'd better warn Ginny. "You should know that I'll probably have a friend with me. You can trust him."

The silence had her checking the phone to make sure the call hadn't disconnected. She placed it back to her ear. "Ginny?"

"If you say so."

"I do. Hang tight. I'm on my way." The call ended. Charlotte stared at her phone, hoping nothing happened to Ginny before she could help the teen.

Now to tell Dennis. She drew in a deep breath and strode into the living room. "I have to meet Ginny, one of the girls I counsel, as soon as possible. I can go by myself, but if you want to go with me, we have to hurry."

Dennis pushed to his feet. His gaze shifted from her to his daughter and back.

Kyle joined him and clapped him on the shoulder. "I've got this, boss. Go."

Dennis's conflicted gaze would have touched her heart if the worry for Ginny hadn't occupied that space.

"Are you sure?" he asked.

The deputy nodded.

Dennis crouched next to Amelia. "I'm sorry, sweetie, but I need to go with Miss Charlotte for a while. Will you be okay with Uncle Kyle?"

"It's okay, Daddy." The little girl threw her arms around her father and squeezed.

The scene playing out in front of Charlotte tugged at her heart. Amelia didn't deserve her hesitance, but she had no time to think about it right now. She had to get to Ginny. "I'm sorry, Amelia, but Theo has to come with me this time."

Amelia kissed the dog's nose. "I'll see you later, Theo."

A small smile tugged on Charlotte's lips. "Theo, *come*." The dog lumbered to her side in protest of leaving his new friend. "Don't worry, boy. We'll be back soon."

Dennis grabbed his keys and coat then held the door open. "Let's go."

She hurried to get her things and follow him out the door. "You don't have to come. I have Theo. Besides, it's only Ginny."

"I'm not in the habit of letting people walk into dangerous situations without backup. Not even when they have a dog."

"Ginny isn't dangerous."

"No, but whoever shot Jordan and took aim at you is." He unlocked the SUV, helped her onto the passenger seat, rounded the vehicle and slid behind the wheel.

He *had* to remind her about that. It still tweaked her that she hadn't remembered the second bullet. But the trauma had shielded her mind. For that, she was grateful. Otherwise, she'd be a basket case.

"Where to?"

"Henry's Gas Station on the outskirts of town."

"Got it." Dennis pulled from his driveway and aimed the vehicle toward the rendezvous point. "I want you to be extra careful when we get there."

She wanted to protest and tell him nothing would happen, but after today, her confidence faltered. "I will. I don't know what Ginny wants, but she was scared."

Dennis's gaze seemed to be everywhere. On the mirrors, down the side streets and back to the mirrors.

"Is there something wrong?" She glanced over her shoulder, searching for anything out of place.

"No."

"Then why do I feel like you're worried someone is following us?"

"I'm not taking any chances. I intend to get you there and back to the house in one piece." A man, all business, had replaced the softer, gentler Dennis.

She'd seen it happen earlier, but sitting next

to him in the SUV sent a shiver up her spine at his intensity. "Thank you for coming with me."

"It's my job."

Ouch. "No, you didn't have to come. You could have sent Kyle and stayed home with your daughter."

His hands tightened on the steering wheel. "She'll be fine with him. The guys are like uncles to her. They've made sure she feels loved and wanted."

"I'm glad you both have them. It must be nice to have the support." Maybe if she'd had that kind of love, her life wouldn't have spiraled out of control.

"You mentioned surviving high school. I take it you didn't have someone in your corner?"

Her laugh had no humor to it. "You could say that." She watched the neighborhoods whiz past. "My mom left when I was five, and my father blamed me. I pretty much fended for myself after that. I'd go to school, then come home and cook and clean."

Dennis's breath caught. "So you grew up like Amelia."

She hadn't really thought of it that way. "I guess I did. But I was five before I had the responsibility thrown on me. Not practically a toddler." Using her own past as an example, she tried to imagine Amelia's life. The thought made Charlotte's heart ache for the child.

"Still. Maybe you can help me figure out how to make sure she knows I won't abandon her."

"Honestly, Dennis, I don't think you have anything to worry about." Charlotte blinked back the tears forming on her lashes. "From what I can tell, she's flourishing under your love."

"That's nice of you to say." He glanced at her then back to the road. "But there are moments when I say the wrong things, and she closes herself off. Those moments don't last long, but there's something hiding deep down that she refuses to tell me about." He exhaled. "I'd really like it if you'd talk with her. Since you understand."

"I don't know, Dennis." She bit her lip. Her training and her experience gave her an edge in relating to the little girl. But could she put her hurt aside? "I'll think about it."

"That's all I ask." He turned into the gas station parking lot. She noticed he'd pulled into a slot near the front entrance but far enough away to have a good view of the whole place. "Where is Ginny planning to meet you?"

"I assume inside. I'll go see if I can find her." Charlotte stepped from the vehicle, only to have Dennis at her side before she closed the passenger door. "I can—"

He held up a hand. "I get it. She'll be more comfortable if I'm not with you. But that doesn't mean I'm not standing watch." He motioned toward the entrance of the store. "Please, stay where I can see you."

"I'll be back with Ginny. I hope." Charlotte rolled down Theo's window. He stuck his head out and licked her cheek. Oh, how she loved that dog. "*Stay*, boy." She straightened her shoulders and strode to the front door. *Come on. Please be close by.* Charlotte peered through the window and spotted Ginny's red hair. A long exhale escaped her lips. She opened the glass door and went inside.

A rack of books hid Ginny from anyone not specifically looking for her. Charlotte strode passed the counter and slipped into the next aisle. "Ginny," Charlotte whispered.

"Miss B?"

"I'm here, honey. Come on. I have someone waiting on us. Let's get you out of here."

Ginny shook her head. "No. They'll find me."

She wrapped the teen in a hug. "Who are you afraid of?"

"I don't know who they are, but I haven't seen Hannah or Stella. I'm really worried that something has happened to them."

Charlotte stiffened. "Why do you say that?"

"Because the other day at Sadie's Place, we talked about our choices. We all had changed our minds and wanted to keep our babies." She rubbed her hand over her belly. "Then they both disappeared."

The girl was obviously scared to death, and for good reason, but for the life of Charlotte, the pieces continued to float around and not connect to complete the full picture.

"Honey, why would that worry you? You can change your mind if you want to. You haven't signed any papers."

"But they're gone!"

"Has someone threatened you?"

Ginny shook her head. "Not yet."

"Calm down." She rubbed Ginny's back. The girl was talking in circles. "I'm happy to sit with you and figure it all out."

Tears trailed down Ginny's cheeks, and she took a deep breath. "Have you heard from Hannah or Stella? I know they trust you. They'd have come to you if they could."

Charlotte's heart shattered into a million pieces. How did she tell the girl about Stella? "I haven't heard from Hannah, but I've seen Stella."

"Oh, good. At least Stella is okay."

"Ginny." Telling the teen about her friend here in the store wasn't a good idea, but keeping it a secret wasn't an option. "I didn't say that." Charlotte waited for Ginny to clue in to what she'd said.

"No!"

Charlotte pulled the teen to her and let her sob on her shoulder. "We have to figure out what's going on. Will you come with me and talk to my friend? His name is Dennis, and he's the sheriff around here. You can trust him."

The warmth of Ginny's tears on Charlotte's neck grew cold when the girl leaned back and stared at her. "You promise?"

"I do." She held out her hand, and Ginny took it. "He's waiting outside."

With a nod for confirmation, Ginny followed Charlotte through the store and into the parking lot.

"I think it'd be a good idea for you to tell us everything you know."

Ginny sniffed. "I can do that."

"Good."

Shoes pounded to Charlotte's left. She turned to see a large man dressed in black charging toward them.

SEVEN

Thursday 2:30 p.m.

The cold air seeped into Dennis's jacket. He jammed his hands in his pockets and hunched his shoulders to block the unwanted discomfort.

Relief flooded him when he spotted the women standing outside the convenience store. Finally. He strode toward them, but Charlotte's reaction puzzled him. A quick glance in the direction of her focus sent panic spiraling through him.

"Watch out!" He sprinted toward her.

A man in black raised his weapon and pulled the trigger.

Dennis tackled Charlotte to the ground, and the bullet shattered the store window, raining glass over them. Breathing hard, he rose and shook off the shards.

Clutching a screaming Ginny, the shooter took off running into the woods next to the gas station.

Charlotte struggled to lift her head. Blood

trickled down her temple and onto her coat. "Ginny!"

Dennis resisted his need to check on Charlotte and pushed to his feet. "Call 911." It was only then that he realized Theo had jumped from the open window of his SUV and bolted after the masked man. Dennis followed the dog that raced after the pregnant teen and her abductor.

"Stop! Police!" He pulled his Glock from his holster.

The masked man whirled around and pointed the barrel of the gun at Ginny's temple, using her as a shield. "Back off!"

Ginny cried out. Her eyes pleaded for help, but there was no way he could use his weapon without putting her in harm's way.

Theo's deep ferocious bark stunned not only Dennis but the assailant.

"Get that dog away from me!" A touch of fear rolled through the man's voice.

"Easy, boy." Dennis prayed Theo's actions wouldn't cause the man to panic and pull the trigger.

The dog maintained his stance and snarled. His barks became low growls.

"Drop your gun, Sheriff." Wide wild eyes peered through the holes in the black ski mask.

Unhinged was Dennis's best description of the man. He fought the urge to comply and instead followed his training and refused to lower his weapon. "You need to let her go."

The guy's eyes darkened a split second before he threw Ginny to the ground and took off through the trees.

"Get him, Theo." He had no idea of the commands, but the dog took off running.

Dennis paused at Ginny's side. "Are you okay? Can you walk?"

Her tearstained face peered up at him. "Yes."

"Go find Charlotte. I'll be back." He hated leaving her, but he didn't want to let the man get away. His Glock in hand, he followed the barking and snapping that led him like runway lights to the attacker.

The masked man lay on the ground, arm up protecting his face. Theo stood over him, looking as though he planned to make a meal of the guy.

"Get him off me!"

Dennis grabbed the guy's weapon and tucked it in his waistband, then aimed his own gun at the perp. "I suggest you don't move." He wasn't sure what Theo would do. He was a SAR dog, not a protection K9. But still. "I've got him, boy. You can sit and relax." He had no idea what to do to make the dog stand down.

Theo stopped, looked at him and tilted his head. After a moment, he sat on his haunches, panting.

"That's it. Good boy."

The attacker moved, and Theo growled.

"I think you better do as you're told. Theo here isn't too happy with you." The man apparently decided to heed the warning and visibly gave up.

"Good. Roll over and put your hands behind your back." Dennis held his stance, gun pointed at the suspect. He didn't trust the man to comply without a fight.

To his surprise, the assailant obeyed.

"Hey, Theo, think you can keep him from running?"

Faster than Dennis registered what had happened, Theo stood over the man with a snarl on his doggy lip.

Cold wind circled around them as Dennis tightened the flex cuffs on the suspect and lifted him to his feet. A quick yank of the ski mask revealed the man's face. As sheriff, Dennis knew almost everyone in the community, at least by sight. But this guy was a mystery.

Theo took the opposite side of the suspect like a sentinel on a mission. Snow and ice crunched beneath their boots on their way back through the woods. Red and blue lights flashed beyond the tree line. Dennis exhaled. His deputies had arrived. He'd hated leaving Charlotte, but knew she had people around her. Plus, she never would have forgiven him if Ginny had gotten hurt.

Dennis, along with the guy in custody and Theo, emerged from the woods. The scene in front of him reminded him of ants at a picnic. He almost chuckled.

When Charlotte called 911, she must have said the sheriff needed help. And help he'd gotten. Five department vehicles lined the parking lot along with an ambulance. Charlotte sat on the bumper of the medic unit, and Ginny sat on the gurney inside while paramedics Rachel and Peter took care of their injuries.

Thank You, Lord, for protecting them.

"Hey, Sheriff." Deputy Tara Fielding, who'd joined the department six months ago, strode over to him.

"Tara. Do you think you can take custody of the assailant for me?"

"Sure thing, sir."

He handed the offender into Deputy Fielding's capable hands. "Get him processed, and I'll meet you at the station when I'm done here."

She gave him a clipped nod and led the criminal to her vehicle.

After taking a deep breath, he proceeded toward the ladies.

"Sheriff Monroe." Keith fell into step next to him. "You should let the paramedics take a look at those injuries before you start directing the investigation."

His forward progress halted. "Excuse me?"

"Those cuts and bruises." Keith pointed to the left side of his face. "At least one looks pretty deep."

He patted his cheek and withdrew his hand. Crimson coated his fingers. Adrenaline had kept him moving without a clue. Now that Keith had pointed it out, he became aware of the blood trickling down his face and the sting that accompanied it. He sighed. "Let's go. I'll fill you in while Rachel cleans up this road rash."

"Rachel?" Keith quirked a brow.

"Not like that, man. You married guys are killing me. She has a gentler touch than Peter. And let's face it, I'm a wimp when it comes to stuff like this."

Keith chuckled. "All right. Rachel it is."

He wanted to smack his deputy on the back of the head but refrained. They were in an official capacity, and he was Keith's boss, not his friend right now. "Lead the way."

A smile curved on Charlotte's lips when she focused on him before she returned her attention to Peter, who was treating her cuts.

Relief hit him hard. He'd worried about his choice of leaving her and Ginny to go after the bad guy, but he'd followed his instinct, and it had paid off. The creep was in custody, and the women appeared shaken from the trauma but okay.

"Sheriff." Rachel approached with a smirk on her face.

"Rachel."

"I'm guessing you want to keep up your manly persona in front of the lady."

His mouth dropped open, then he closed his eyes for a second and shook his head. "I would think being sheriff would get me a little respect around here." He gave her a playful glare. "Why couldn't Brent and Ethan be on duty?"

She crossed her arms. "They do get to leave the firehouse once in a while, you know. Besides, I'm the one with the lollipops."

He pretended to ponder her words. "Well, there is that."

"Come on. Let's get those cuts cleaned and Steri-Stripped closed."

Feeling like a little boy dragging his feet, he followed her to the passenger seat of Keith's SUV and plopped down.

"Would you stop pouting? I promise I'll be gentle."

"Yeah, yeah, so you say." Dennis loved the banter. He wasn't the wimp they made him out to be, but the whole thing had taken on a life of its own after he'd wrecked his mountain bike a couple of years ago.

While Rachel wiped the blood from his face and removed slivers of glass from his skin, he peered over her shoulder at Charlotte. She'd climbed into the ambulance next to Ginny and held the girl's hand.

He flinched when Rachel pulled the edges of his cut together to secure it closed.

"Hold still."

"I am."

"Are not." She tsked and added the strips. "There we go. All done." She dug into her bag and pulled out an instant ice pack. With a quick smack, she broke the chemicals inside and shook it. "Here. Put that on those bruises. You really did a number on yourself."

"Hitting the ground hard and having glass rain down on you will do that."

"I suppose." Rachel held out a cherry lollipop.

He lifted a brow. "What, I don't get to choose?"

With an exasperated sigh, she fanned out several flavors and stared at him. "Which one then?"

"Cherry." He smiled.

"You're an absolute brat."

He snatched the candy and grinned. "Yup."

"Go before I take it back." Rachel flicked her fingers like swatting a gnat.

"I'm out." He plucked two more lollipops from her hand.

"Hey!"

"I have to take a peace offering to the ladies."

Rachel shook her head and stuffed her supplies into her bag.

Dennis pushed from the seat and instantly regretted sitting down. His muscles hated him and protested the movement. Between the injuries during the snowstorm and two different tackles to the ground, he felt every one of his thirty-eight years. Clenching his teeth until the stiffness dissipated, he shuffled over to Charlotte.

He leaned against the door of the ambulance. "How's everyone doing?"

Charlotte shifted her attention to him. "We're good. Only minor scrapes and bruises." She narrowed her gaze. "Better than you."

"Ouch." He grimaced. He looked *that* bad?

Her hand flew to her mouth. "I'm so sorry."

"It's okay. I have a feeling I'd say the same if I looked into a mirror." He held out the lollipops. "I come bearing gifts."

With a laugh, Charlotte took them and handed one to Ginny. "Thanks."

He hadn't noticed Theo's presence until the dog pressed his head against Charlotte's knee. Dennis pointed to Theo. "He's amazing. I didn't think SAR dogs were trained to apprehend a suspect."

"They aren't, but someone shot at me, and he knows Ginny. He's protective of those he likes. He must like you too, since he decided to leave Ginny and help you."

"Whatever the reason, he deserves a big treat."

Theo lifted his head at the word *treat*. Charlotte rubbed between his ears. "As soon as we get out of here, I'll make sure he gets a nice reward."

"Good. He earned it."

"The paramedics said we are free to go since we refused a trip to the hospital."

Dennis straightened. "Are you sure that's a good idea?" He motioned toward Ginny.

"I'm fine, Sheriff. My blood pressure is normal, and the baby's heartbeat is strong." The young lady sounded okay, but he didn't want to take any chances with her health.

If the girl was anything like Charlotte, he knew not to argue.

"I'm glad to hear that. I was worried when you fell back there."

Charlotte bit her lip. "I don't like the idea of Ginny being alone—"

"Say no more." Dennis called over Deputy DJ Lewis.

DJ jogged to join them. "Yes, sir."

"I'd like you to escort Miss Ginny to the station for her statement, then back to Sadie's Place. Plan to stay and monitor who comes and goes. I'll send someone to relieve you in a few hours."

"Will do." The deputy nodded and turned to the teen. "Miss Ginny, are you ready to go?"

Ginny scooted to the edge of the gurney, and DJ helped her out of the ambulance. She pivoted to face Dennis. "Thank you, Sheriff Monroe."

He nodded. "Take care of yourself and that baby."

She ran a protective hand over her belly and smiled. "I will."

Dennis watched as the pair left the scene, then shifted his attention to Charlotte. "What about you? Want to get out of here?"

"I'm more than ready."

He held out a hand. She took it and eased to the ground. Theo hopped down next to her. "I have to go to the station. I'll take you back to my place if you want, and get your statement later, but I'd rather not."

She stopped, causing him to turn around. "My statement? Why?"

"Charlotte. That man tried to shoot you."

The wind stirred and whipped hair across her face. With a shaky hand, she brushed the strands from her eyes. "But he was after Ginny. He grabbed her, not me."

If only that were the case. Dennis grasped her hands in his. "Yes, he took Ginny, but make no mistake, he tried to kill you first." He hated his blunt words, but she had to understand the danger. "Someone wants you dead."

Theo pushed against her leg and whined. She

absently stroked the dog's fur. "But why?" Her voice quivered.

He had no clue, but the more time he spent with Charlotte, the more desperate he became to solve that mystery. "That is what I intend to find out."

After Charlotte gave her statement, Dennis escorted her and Theo to the station conference room with a promise to return soon.

Heat flowed from the vents, but the warm air hadn't chased away the chill. Maybe because Charlotte's shivers had nothing to do with the temperature.

Someone wants you dead.

Dennis's words echoed in her head. Why would someone want to kill her? She reached down and ran a hand over a sleeping Theo. He raised his head, then laid his snout on his front paws with a huff.

The door opened, and Deputy Lewis escorted Ginny in and helped her into a seat.

"What's going on, Miss B?" Ginny sniffed.

"I don't know, honey. I wish I did." Charlotte knelt beside the teen. "Are you okay?"

The girl rubbed her belly. "Yes. I just want to know why that man grabbed me."

"I'm sure Sheriff Monroe will get to the bottom of it." She rose and had to wait for her aching muscles to catch up with her action. "Is there anything you can tell me that will help us find Hannah?"

A sob caught in Ginny's throat. "They told me about Stella. Did you really find her?"

"I did. I'm sorry. The two of you and Hannah were close."

Deputy Lewis handed Ginny a tissue, and she wiped her eyes. "I can't believe they took her baby."

Yeah, that baffled Charlotte too. "You told me earlier that all three of you changed your minds about giving your babies up for adoption."

The teen nodded. "Hannah's parents promised to help her until she and Jordan figured out what they wanted to do. And Stella…" She hiccupped a sob. "Her parents wanted nothing to do with her, but when her grandparents called her a few days ago, they asked her to come live with them so she could finish school."

Charlotte had helped Stella reach out to her grandparents but hadn't heard that they'd made an offer to take her in. "What about you?" The changes in the girls' decisions were news to Charlotte too. Although, with the exception of Hannah, she hadn't met with the teens for a couple of weeks, and a lot could change in that amount of time.

"I don't know what I'm going to do, but I just

can't go through with it. At least not right now."
Tears rolled down Ginny's cheeks and off her
chin.

Charlotte clutched the girl's hand and squeezed.
"We'll figure it out. Together."

Deputy Lewis maintained his position in the
corner, letting them talk without interruption.
Quiet descended, and neither woman said anything for a long while.

"Ginny, who else knew you all had changed
your minds?"

The teen swallowed hard. "No one. Well…
maybe our social worker."

Charlotte straightened in her seat. "Erin Rivers?"

"Yes. We didn't exactly tell her, but she walked
in on us talking in the lounge."

A knock on the door had Theo on alert. "Easy,
boy."

Dennis peeked his head in. "May I join you?"

"Sure." She motioned for him to sit.

He dropped into a chair and ran his fingers
through his hair. "We hit a dead end with your
attacker."

"What?" The blood whooshed in Charlotte's
ears.

"The man's name is Hank James. He's not the
one in charge. In fact, he doesn't know the person
who hired him. It was all done over the phone,
and the money was a cash drop."

"So we're no closer to finding out who's after us or to finding Hannah?" All her hopes of the threats ending vanished.

"I'm sorry, Charlotte. I promise we aren't backing off. We'll continue to investigate."

She wanted to kick and scream at the unfairness of it all, but she sucked in a breath and turned to Deputy Lewis. "Please take Ginny back to Sadie's Place. She's had a long day. And I'd appreciate it if you'd keep an eye on her."

The teen gave her a forced smile. "I'd really like that."

"Will do, Ms. Bradley. Come on, Miss Ginny." The deputy cupped the girl's elbow and escorted her out of the conference room.

Once the door closed, Charlotte dropped her head into her hands. "I can't believe this." Theo nudged his nose between her arms and licked her cheek. She held his snout and kissed his head, then buried her face in his fur.

"Charlotte." Dennis's soft voice tugged at her heart.

He hadn't left her side since the chaos started. Even when she'd kept her distance from Amelia. He'd put his life in danger to protect her. The man deserved more than a bad attitude toward his daughter. "I'm sorry."

"This whole situation isn't your fault."

She shook her head but didn't correct him. Her

grandpa had always told her that actions spoke louder than words. Which she found out at age twenty when she'd announced her pregnancy, and her father had shunned her. His message had come across loud and clear. Not that he'd really cared about her anyway.

She rubbed her eyes with her forefinger and thumb. "Can we go now?"

He studied her for a moment and stood. "We're done here. I'll take you back to my place. If you're up for it, my deputies are coming over to review the evidence and talk through the case. I'd like for you to join us."

"I'm willing to help any way I can. Hannah is still missing, and something strange is going on. I want answers." She snapped on the dog's leash. "Come on, Theo." Once they arrived at the house, she'd feed him and let him out to roam in the backyard.

Dennis waved goodbye to his administrative assistant, Brenda, and led Charlotte out the main entrance. He placed a protective hand on the small of her back while his other hand hovered over his weapon.

She hadn't missed the tension rolling off him. "You think there's someone else out there?"

"I do. Hank is low-hanging fruit. He was in it for the money, nothing else." Dennis opened the passenger door, and she slid in. "I don't want to scare you, but whoever has you in his sights isn't giving up." The door snicked shut.

He didn't want to scare her? Too late for that. Charlotte wasn't scared—she was terrified.

EIGHT

After a trip through a local drive-thru for dinner, and him and Charlotte scarfing it down in the truck, Dennis strolled into his house and followed his nose to the kitchen. Cookies filled the kitchen table and flour coated the countertops, but he didn't mind the mess. His daughter had made him a treat, and he'd enjoy it.

"I see Amelia's been at it again." Dennis sampled one of the chocolate chip cookies and groaned. "And she's found the perfect recipe."

"You really think so, Daddy?" His daughter threw her arms around his neck and kissed his cheek.

"I do. These are the best ones yet." He raised a brow at Kyle.

His deputy cringed. "She can be very persuasive."

Dennis chuckled. That was an understatement. "Tell ya what, princess. Why don't you put a bunch of those on a plate, and we'll give the others an opportunity to taste your baking."

Amelia smiled and hurried to her task. She brushed flour from the apron she'd begged him to buy her several weeks ago. The powder drifted to the floor, adding to the already-white dusting. He knew she'd clean her mess, but he'd make sure her duties stopped with the baking or at least that she had help with the disaster that was now his kitchen.

"You're not mad?" Kyle whispered.

Dennis almost laughed out loud at his friend's surprise. "No. My girl is happy. That's what counts." And he truly meant it. Dennis wasn't naive. He couldn't let her get away with everything, but for now, he'd give her a little extra space to explore childhood. Something she hadn't had much of—if any.

"I'll help clean up."

Dennis spun to see Charlotte push up her sleeves and walk toward the table. Had she just volunteered to spend time with Amelia? "That's okay. I can do it later."

"No, it's fine. Theo is happily relaxing in the backyard, and we girls need time to get to know each other."

He had to admit, Charlotte appeared a bit stiff, but she made an effort to be with his daughter.

"All right. When you're finished, please join us in the living room."

She nodded and stepped next to Amelia. "Let's see if we can arrange these cookies in a nice pile on the plate before we clean up."

"I've tried, but they look like a mess." Amelia huffed and pointed to the tower tumbling from the plate.

"Come on. I'll show you how." Charlotte moved to the sink and washed her hands. "You see, Amelia, you can't stack them on top of each other. You have to think pyramid."

Wow. What had just happened? Dennis shook the confusion from his brain and left his daughter in Charlotte's hands.

The doorbell rang, and he made his way to the entry, shaking off the weird event he'd witnessed. Chatter filled his house as his friends filed in and took up residence in the living room.

"Thanks for coming, everyone." Dennis lowered himself into the recliner the guys had left for him.

"Anytime." Keith sat next to Amy on the couch and draped his arm over her shoulders.

"Where's Carter tonight?" Carter, Keith's almost one-year-old son, whom he'd found out about a little over six months ago—and Amy's nephew, now her son too since the of murder of her twin—was cherished by both.

Dennis had to admit the little guy had every member of the department wrapped around his finger.

Amy smiled at Keith. "With his grandpa Ian."

The fact that Keith and Amy had agreed to leave the boy and come help spoke volumes about their friendship with Dennis. "Ian must be loving having Carter."

"He practically threw us out of the house." Keith chuckled. "Dad likes being a grandpa."

Amy's lip twitched at the understatement. Ian loved the grandparent gig.

Jason maneuvered around the couch and dropped a box on the floor. "Is the coffee table okay?" His gaze drifted to the kitchen and back.

"It's fine. We'll just keep the graphic pictures tucked out of sight in case Amelia comes in." He appreciated his friend's concern. Dennis scratched the stubble on his jaw. "She's a smart one. I try not to talk about work around her, but she overhears grown-ups talking at school or when we run errands around town, and she asks me pointed questions. I vowed to myself and her that I'll never lie to her." The times he smoothed over the truth, she'd glare at him and call him out on it.

"I can't believe she's only in kindergarten." Melanie took her usual position on the floor with Jason behind her on the couch.

Kyle and Doug dragged several more chairs in and sat down. Kyle flipped his around and straddled it. "That girl read me a Nancy Drew mystery the other day. And I couldn't believe it when she explained it to me." He smirked. "Taking after her father already."

"Not in the IQ department." Dennis shook his head. "What am I going to do when she's in high school?"

The group laughed and gave him a bit of good-natured ribbing.

"Miss Charlotte and I have treats and coffee," Amelia announced as she waltzed in with a plate stacked high with cookies and put them on the coffee table.

"Amelia's responsible for the goodies. I'm only the bearer of beverages." Charlotte placed the cups and carafe next to the treats.

"Thank you, Amelia." Doug leaned forward and snatched three cookies as Jason protested the quick move.

Dennis's daughter brought him a napkin with two. "Here, Daddy."

"Thanks, princess." He kissed her cheek, and she smiled.

"May I go read on the back porch? Theo's out there, and he's lonely."

"Is he now?"

She bit her lip and nodded.

"Sure. Go on. Bundle up. It's cold out there. And don't leave the yard."

Amelia rolled her eyes in a very teenage dramatic fashion. "Yes, Daddy." With a quick hug, she skipped from the room.

Charlotte's gaze followed his daughter's path. If he wasn't mistaken, tension had melted off the woman like a spring thaw.

"Time to get down to business if y'all are done feeding your faces." Melanie lifted the lid on the box and handed Jason an envelope.

Jason playfully glared at his wife, then removed a stack of photos. "These are the images from the crime scene. I didn't see anything of note that will help us but thought it was worth taking another look." He passed the first picture around the room. "That one is the area around the body."

Each person studied the image before passing it on. They did the same for the next twenty photos. None triggered any specific information.

"And this one is of Stella's medallion." Jason handed it off and collected the other pictures that had made their way around.

Charlotte's brow furrowed. "Wait. That's not Stella's. Or at least I don't think it is."

"Whose is it then?" Jason asked.

Melanie held up a hand. "Hold on. The lab rats cleaned it up."

Dennis shook his head. "When are you going to quit calling your assistants that?"

"Psh. They love it." Melanie dug through the box. "Found it." She passed the plastic bag across the table to Charlotte.

Two fingers holding the edge of the baggie like it would jump out and bite her, Charlotte narrowed her gaze. "No. That's not Stella's."

Kyle straightened. "The killer's?"

"Maybe." Charlotte's eyes met his.

Dennis wanted to reach over and smooth the crease from her forehead but refrained and waited for her to speak. When she didn't, he decided to prod. "What is it, Charlotte?"

She pinched her lips and exhaled. "I'm pretty sure I've seen it before."

"Where?"

"It looks familiar, but that's just it, I can't remember where." She handed the evidence back to Melanie. "Who knows? Maybe I saw it on TV."

Dennis highly doubted it. Something had prompted Charlotte's memory.

The group spent another thirty minutes discussing the images and evidence. During that time, Amelia had come in and headed to her bedroom with a happy Theo in tow. Maybe he *should* get his daughter a dog. Dennis mentally shook the reoccurring thought away. He had to quit wanting to give Amelia everything.

Putting the idea on hold, he rubbed the back of his neck, trying to relieve the tension.

The team talked over each other, throwing out ideas, making his head hurt.

He cleared his throat. "Let's back up for a minute. Mel and her lab rats will continue to work on the body and evidence side. I want to figure out why the girls and Charlotte are being targeted."

Doug shifted in his chair to face Charlotte. "Have the teens said anything? Any clue at all?"

"Well..." Charlotte placed her fingertips over her mouth and closed her eyes, appearing deep in thought.

The room became silent except for the crackle of the fire in the fireplace and the hum of the refrigerator in the kitchen.

Her eyes opened, and she shrugged. "According to Ginny, all three had changed their minds about the adoptions and planned to keep their babies. But that's all I can think of. I haven't talked to Stella and Ginny in a couple of weeks."

"Did anyone else know this?"

"Not that I'm aware of. I didn't even know, and they tend to tell me everything." Charlotte snapped her fingers. "Wait a second. Ginny told me they thought Erin Rivers might have overheard the conversation."

"Is that a bad thing?" Doug asked.

"Not as far as I'm concerned. Erin's a friend.

She cares about these girls." Charlotte pinched the bridge of her nose. "But I'm at a loss here."

"So back to the girls." Dennis refocused the discussion. "They changed their minds, and now everything has gone haywire."

"Why would someone target a girl for changing her mind?" Amy grumbled. "That doesn't make sense." Amy's words halted everyone in the room, and they all stared at her. "What did I say?"

Kyle looked at Dennis. "You don't think, do you?"

"I don't know what to think right now. But I'd like to talk with the attorney."

Charlotte and Amy gave him a look that questioned his sanity.

Charlotte spoke first. "Apparently, Amy and I don't have investigative minds. Someone want to tell us what just happened?"

Leaning forward, Dennis rested his elbows on his knees. "What if the person or persons after these teens had plans for those babies, and the girls are messing that up?"

Charlotte's jaw dropped. "You mean those men sold the babies?"

He cringed. It sounded so harsh, but life had no guarantees that things would be easy. He should know. Look at Amelia. A social worker had dropped her off with him and walked away.

Suddenly he was a father with a five-year-old daughter. A daughter who had suffered at the hands of her mother, then been left with a man she didn't know. He drew in a deep breath. "It's a theory, but it could be wrong."

"So the bad guy is out to take the babies." Charlotte slumped in her seat. "But why try to kill me?"

Once again, silence hovered over the room.

Jason snapped his fingers. "The medallion."

"I'm not following." Charlotte stared at the man.

"You recognize it," Kyle added.

"Sure, but I have no idea why."

Jason tag-teamed with Kyle. "The killer doesn't know that."

The blood drained from Charlotte's face, leaving it a pasty white that worried Dennis. "It makes sense."

"Maybe it's not related to the evidence but the fact he thinks you saw him out in the woods." Dennis shrugged.

"But I didn't."

Jason held his palms out. "Again, he doesn't know that."

Charlotte swallowed hard. Her gaze drifted to the window. "What if he's out there watching? Waiting."

If Dennis were honest, he worried about the same thing.

Lord, how am I supposed to find a missing girl and a newborn, protect two unborn babies and keep Charlotte safe? Then there's Amelia. I don't want her in the middle of this.

The weight of the world had dropped and landed squarely on his shoulders.

Wonderful. Charlotte's life was in danger, and she had no idea where the threat came from.

A lump clogged her throat. Falling apart in front of these people didn't sit well with her. They all exuded strength and courage, and here she was on the verge of becoming a blubbering mess. She excused herself and rushed to the kitchen before the tears fell.

Fingers gripping the edge of the sink, Charlotte hung her head and struggled to catch her breath. Hadn't she lived through enough pain in her life with her mother's abandonment and her father kicking her out when she got pregnant? Not to mention, the father of her baby had wanted nothing to do with her as soon as he'd found out about the pregnancy. Then to top it all off, her baby died while she lay in the hospital alone. *God, where were You when I needed You most?*

"What can I do to help?" The deep baritone of Dennis's voice signaled he stood a few feet away.

Why did he have to be so nice? She shook her head when her voice refused to function.

A paper napkin appeared in front of her. "Here."

"Thank you," she whispered.

"Want to tell me what's going on?"

She shrugged. Not ready to share, she went with the obvious. "Being a target for a killer is messing with my mind. I keep coming back to why."

"I think the group is correct. The attacker thinks you can identify him. Either from the medallion or simply because you found Stella."

Charlotte straightened and shifted her gaze to him. His gray eyes held so much compassion that her legs almost failed her.

"After seeing the medallion, has anything clicked?"

"No. Nothing more than a familiarity that I can't explain." Charlotte rubbed her temples. "What if it's the answer to Hannah's location?"

"We'll find her." He brushed his hand down her arm, sending butterflies loose in her stomach. "I just want you to keep thinking about where you've seen that medallion."

"I promise—" Her cell phone buzzed, and she glanced at the caller ID. "I need to take this."

Dennis nodded and headed back to the living room to give her privacy.

Charlotte answered. "Hi, Ginny."

"Miss B." Ginny sniffed. "I'm scared."

"Talk to me, honey." Charlotte's mind ran wild with horrible scenarios.

"I'm at the hospital. I don't want to have this baby by myself."

Charlotte's hand tightened on her phone. "You're in labor?"

"Yes," the girl cried.

"I'm on my way, Ginny. Hang in there." The timing couldn't be worse with everything going on, but babies didn't ask for permission. They came when they were ready, and Charlotte had vowed not to let her girls go through the experience alone.

"Thank you, Miss B."

The call disconnected.

She shoved the phone into her pocket and rushed to the living room. "I have to get to the hospital." Seven sets of eyes landed on her.

"What's going on?" Dennis's demeanor switched from easygoing to all cop.

"Ginny's in labor and wants me there. I don't want to leave her alone like I... Never mind." She shook her head. No, she'd keep her sad story to herself. She grabbed her coat and froze. Theo. The hospital wouldn't let him come in. What was she supposed to do with her dog?

The hum of voices buzzed in the background as her mind spun in multiple different directions.

A jingle of keys shook her from her thoughts.

"Jason and Mel will stay with Amelia and Theo while the others continue to investigate." He placed a hand on her arm. "Trust me, they'll take good care of your dog."

How had he read her mind? She turned to the couple who sat on the couch. "Are you sure?"

"Go, everything will be fine." Jason tugged his wife closer. "We'll stay and play with your pup and eat all Dennis's food."

Dennis rolled his eyes and held his hand out, motioning toward the door. "If you're ready…"

She slipped on her jacket and hurried to his SUV.

Pulling from the drive, Dennis aimed the vehicle toward town. "Is Ginny okay?"

"From what I can tell, she's just scared." Charlotte squeezed her hands together, thinking about her own experience. Alone and terrified. Just like Ginny.

"It's times like this I wish I lived closer to downtown."

At the moment, she agreed with him. She focused on the trees whipping by and the houses that dotted the county road. "Thanks for taking me. I could have driven, but with everything that's happened, I feel better not being by myself."

"I'm happy to help." His eyes shifted to the rearview mirror, and his hands tightened on the steering wheel.

Goose bumps pricked her skin. "Dennis?"

He jabbed the speed dial on his SUV navigation screen. The phone rang twice.

"Howard."

"Kyle, I need backup," Dennis commanded. "Dark blue sedan on my tail."

"Doug, boss needs help." Kyle's voice filtered through the car. "On our way, Sheriff."

Charlotte shifted and caught sight of a vehicle gaining on them. If danger hadn't followed them, she'd laugh at the quick way the deputies shifted from friend to employee.

The line stayed open. A door slammed, and the sound of heavy breathing and footfalls filled the interior of the SUV.

"Three minutes, boss."

"Got it." Dennis glanced at her, then back at the road. "They'll get here in time. Besides, I have a few tricks of my own."

Of course he did. He was the sheriff after all. But still. Her mind told her he'd get them to the hospital without incident, but her heart pounded at a thunderous rate.

"One minute," Kyle announced, bringing her back from her wayward thoughts.

Charlotte's fingernails dug into the edge of the seat. "He must be flying."

Dennis's chuckle matched Kyle's.

"I learned from the best," Kyle said.

"How can the two of you laugh at a time like this?" Her words had a bite that she hadn't intended. The two men were calm, and she was a nervous mess.

Dennis sat up straighter, his gaze scanning the road ahead. "Main Street is coming up. I'm going in the opposite direction of the hospital and will circle back around. Give this guy a distraction."

"Copy that, Sheriff."

"Hold on, Charlotte." Dennis whipped the SUV to the left.

The car followed his maneuver and decreased the distance between them.

"Now what? He's still there and getting closer." She wanted to tell Dennis to stop the car so she could march over to the guy and demand answers. She exhaled. Yup, the whole situation had stolen her common sense and replaced it with lunacy.

"Wait for it." Dennis sped up, expanding the distance when Kyle swerved in between them and the offending vehicle. "Thanks for the assist."

Kyle moved to block both lanes of traffic. "Now."

Dennis whipped around the next corner and sped toward the hospital.

The squeal of tires erupted over the phone line. Several agonizing minutes later, Dennis drummed his fingers on the steering wheel. "Update."

"Sorry, Sheriff, he got away."

Charlotte rubbed her eyes and sighed.

"Thanks for trying, Kyle. Tell Jason to stay vigilant and keep Amelia safe. I don't know exactly where I picked up that tail, and that worries me."

"Will do. And by the way, Doug headed straight to the hospital and is keeping watch." Kyle disconnected.

"You don't think whoever is after me will go after your daughter, do you?" Charlotte hadn't considered that staying with him would put his little family in danger.

Dennis stretched his neck from side to side and let the silence linger. He finally shook his head. "No, I don't. But I'm not taking any chances."

Smart move on his part. Nothing about the situation seemed to follow any rules.

A few moments later, he pulled into the hospital parking lot and stopped at the space reserved for law enforcement. He gave a small salute to his deputy Doug, who sat in his truck outside the entrance.

"Stay put." He stepped from the vehicle and rounded the front of the SUV. His eyes in constant movement, looking for trouble. Door open, he held out his hand, and she accepted. "I want you inside, so let's hurry."

The mild-mannered man she first met had transformed into a no-nonsense sheriff with protection on his mind. Any other time, she'd have found the shift fascinating, but right now, she just appreciated it.

She exited the SUV and matched him stride for stride as they entered the hospital and hurried to the labor and delivery department two floors up.

They spotted Deputy DJ Lewis pacing down the hall and hurried to him.

"How is she?" Dennis asked.

"In labor. But she's safe."

Dennis patted his deputy. "Thanks for taking care of her. Go on, take a break. I've got this."

DJ glanced at Ginny's door. "Keep me posted."

"Will do." After his deputy strode away, Dennis pivoted to face her. "Go on. I'll stand guard. Either Doug or I will be right outside the room."

She rested her hand on his arm. "I can't thank you enough." Giving him a quick smile, she slipped into Ginny's room.

"Miss B, you came." Ginny grimaced as a contraction hit.

"I'm here, honey. I'm not leaving." She took the teen's hand and coached her through the pain. If only someone had been there for her five years ago, maybe she wouldn't have fallen as deep into the emotional agony and grief as she had. Maybe then looking at Dennis's five-year-old daughter wouldn't rip her heart to shreds.

Twelve hours later, tears streamed down Charlotte's cheeks as she held the seven-pound baby girl. "Hey, little one, it's time to meet your momma." She placed the bundle in Ginny's out-stretched arms.

The teen snuggled the newborn and kissed the top of her head. "Thank you for staying." Ginny's words wobbled.

"Ah, honey. No one should go through having a baby alone." She brushed Ginny's sweat-matted hair off her forehead.

Ginny tucked her baby in tight. "Don't let them take her."

"It's okay to change your mind. She's yours. No one can make you sign those papers."

"But what about Stella?" Her question came out on a sob.

Charlotte's mind shifted to the conversation she'd had with the deputies. What if someone was out to take the babies? A strong desire to ask the adoption attorney who worked with Sadie's Place a few questions hit her. "I'll call your social worker to come stay with you and keep anyone from pressuring you to sign the termination-of-parental-rights papers."

Ginny's eyes widened. "Why can't you stay?"

"I need to go see Mr. Kent." Dennis had mentioned the possibility of the lawyer being involved earlier, but Charlotte had brushed it off. Now, she had a few questions of her own.

"All right, I guess." Ginny's shoulders sagged as though she'd given up.

Charlotte placed the call to Erin, and her friend promised to be there in twenty minutes. Had she made a mistake in trusting Erin? Ginny had said that the only person privy to the conversation about keeping the babies was their social worker. And Charlotte couldn't forget the argument between Erin and Mr. Kent at Sadie's Place. She shook off the line of thought and focused on the teen who held her precious baby in her arms. There was no way her friend was involved.

Erin arrived, and after Charlotte passed on the information and voiced her concerns about Ginny's safety, she strode to the waiting area. Tears once more streaked down her face. She grabbed the wall to steady herself as sobs racked her body.

"Charlotte." Dennis wrapped his arms around her, and she buried her face in his chest and let the emotions pour out. He held her tight, rubbing circles on her back.

When she thought she'd cried out her final tears, they kept coming.

"You're kind of worrying me here." He smoothed a hand down her hair. "What happened? Are Ginny and the baby okay?"

She sucked in several shuttering breaths and eased from his embrace. "It's a girl. She's so beautiful. Just like Kayley."

His brow scrunched. "Who's Kayley?"

"My daughter."

Dennis jerked as though she'd slapped him. "You have a daughter?"

"No." She shook her head. The pressure behind her eyes exploded into a full-blown headache. "She died a few hours after I had her. They took her away, and I never got to see her again."

"Ah, Charlotte, I'm so sorry. Come here." He led her to a chair in the waiting room and sat next to her.

She wanted so badly to tell him everything about her pregnancy, her love and loss, but she held back. Admitting what happened to her baby was enough. Especially knowing his experience with Amelia's mother.

No way would she admit to living on the streets after her father had thrown her out or how she got pregnant to begin with.

Secrets. Dennis hated them. And Charlotte seemed to have plenty. But the torture in her eyes crushed him. From what she *had* told him, the woman had experienced more than her share of pain.

His shoulders drooped as the whole situation came into focus. "So that's why you don't like being around Amelia."

"Yes."

He exhaled. What did he say to that?

"She would have been five tomorrow." Charlotte swallowed hard. "It's not that I don't like your daughter. She's an amazing child. It's only that she reminds me of what I lost."

"Why didn't you tell me sooner?" he whispered.

"I'm sorry." The pain etched in her features wormed its way into his heart.

"I shouldn't have said anything. It's none of my business." But he wanted it to be. And that's where the problem lay. Even with all the red flags, he was falling for Charlotte. He shifted to face her and lifted her chin with his fingers. The anguish in her eyes undid him. His gaze drifted to her lips and lingered. He only had to lean in to close the distance.

Voices in the hallway snapped him back to reality. He sat back and cleared his throat. "How's Ginny?"

Disappointment flittered across Charlotte's face, then vanished. "She's doing well. I called Erin to sit with her since we don't know the attacker's endgame."

"It's probably a good idea to have someone with her."

"I'd like to pay a visit to the law office that's handling the adoptions. If what you all said earlier about babies being sold is true, they might have information we need. Or someone there is involved."

"That was on our to-do list of interviews, but I'm not sure I want you out in the open."

"Dennis, I'm in the middle of this whether I want to be or not."

"True." Dennis rubbed the back of his neck, pondering her comment. "The attorney is Troy Kent, I assume."

She nodded.

He'd heard of the man but hadn't had many dealings with him. Although he seemed like an upstanding guy, minus the argument they'd overheard at Sadie's Place. But Dennis had no clue what that had been about. "What's your take on him?"

"He's always treated the girls well. It started out as a family-run office, but he has several partners now. They have an administrative assistant, and Troy's wife, Donna, helps out too." She threw up her hands. "I don't know. Maybe we're on the wrong track."

"No. It's a good idea. And like I said, we planned to interview him anyway." He laced his fingers with hers. The warmth, along with the flutter in his belly, was an odd sensation for him. A woman hadn't affected him like this in a long time. Yes, she'd admitted the reason for her aversion to Amelia, but that was a far cry from fixing the problem, and Charlotte was still holding something back. No matter how he felt, Amelia came first, even though the woman beside him had awakened the want for a wife.

Charlotte let go of Dennis, swiped a hand down her face and straightened. "With Erin here to watch out for Ginny, why don't we go ask our questions?"

"Are you sure you don't want to sleep first? You've had a long night."

"I'm tired, but I'll rest better once we get some answers." Charlotte looked ready to fold. He wanted to push for her to sleep but understood her desire to meet with the attorney first.

Even though he'd stayed at the hospital, he'd catnapped while Doug kept watch during the early parts of the morning. A presence his department would maintain until they got to the bottom of this investigation.

A quick glance at his watch said the law office had opened an hour ago. "Sounds like a plan." He pushed from his seat and offered his hand to help her stand.

Charlotte took it, stood and wobbled.

He gripped her elbow to steady her. "Easy there."

"I'm a little more tired and sore than I thought."

"Trust me, I get it." He smiled. His injuries had made their presence known when he'd woken up from a nap a few hours ago. "I'll get in touch with Jason and Mel and fill them in. Then we'll head to Kent's office."

She didn't respond, only walked next to him while he placed the call. Check-in complete, they strode through the exit to his SUV. He held the door open for her, and she slid in. Once in the driver's seat, Dennis started the engine to warm up the vehicle, then turned to face her. She had her arms folded tightly, fighting off the cold. "It'll be warm soon."

"Just wish soon was now."

He chuckled. "I'll agree with that one." He pursed his lips. There was so much he wanted to say. Where did he start? "Charlotte."

She shifted in her seat to give him her attention. "Yes."

"I'm sorry about what happened to you."

"I—it's life, I guess." She shrugged.

"Doesn't make it hurt any less."

She nodded.

He took a deep breath, debating whether to say more. "I remember when Tina told me that she'd miscarried. Part of me was relieved. I was in college and not ready to be a father. But another part... My heart ached at the loss. If I hurt that badly, I can only imagine what you went through."

Charlotte placed a hand on his arm. A sad smile graced her lips. "Thank you for understanding."

He patted her hand, then shifted the SUV into Reverse and pulled out of the parking spot. "Why don't you catch a power nap while I drive?" She needed the rest, and he needed time to process their conversation and the implications of letting his heart get involved.

"I think I will, if you don't mind."

"Not at all."

Charlotte leaned her head against the window and closed her eyes.

Before he made it out of the parking lot, her body had relaxed and her breathing had evened out.

He yawned and struggled to keep his eyes open as he maneuvered through town. The past day and a half had caught up with him. His body craved a break. Unfortunately, this case required his attention.

Twenty minutes later, he turned into the parking lot of Troy Kent's law office that the man shared with three other attorneys. Dennis cut the engine and jostled Charlotte. "Time to wake up."

She rubbed her eyes and sat up straight. "Wow, I actually slept."

"I'm glad." Dennis palmed his keys. "Are you ready to see Mr. Kent?"

"More than."

A soft ding sounded as they entered the office.

"Good morning." The cheerful words from the receptionist made him cringe.

After staying up most of the night, a cup of coffee or ten might give him the energy to reciprocate, but he forced a smile. "Good morning…" He glanced at the nameplate on her desk. "Penny."

"What can I do for you?"

He flipped his wallet open to his badge and held it up. "Sheriff Dennis Monroe. Is Mr. Kent here? I have a few questions for him."

Charlotte eyed him and raised a brow.

Okay, so maybe flashing his ID was a bit much, but he didn't have time to mess around. Teens and babies were in trouble, and he was tired. His patience had hit an all-time low.

"Yes, he's here, Sheriff. I'll let him know you'd like to speak with him."

"Thank you."

Penny rounded her desk and motioned toward the four soft chairs by the front window. "Please, have a seat."

Dennis paced around the small reception area

while Charlotte all but collapsed into a chair. He made a mental note to head home as soon as they finished to get some shut-eye.

"Sheriff."

He whirled around. "Mr. Kent?"

"Yes." Troy Kent strode forward and offered his hand. Dennis accepted the gesture. "Penny said you have questions for me."

Charlotte stood and joined them. "Mr. Kent, I'm Charlotte Bradley. I counsel the girls at Sadie's Place."

The attorney's gaze softened. "Yes, yes. Nice to see you again, Ms. Bradley. You're doing a wonderful job from what I've been told."

"Thank you, sir. I have a few concerns that I'd like to discuss with you."

Dennis watched as Charlotte transformed from vulnerable to a take-charge professional woman. She'd amazed him from the minute she saved his life during the snowstorm, but it surprised him she had it in her to make the shift after the emotional experience at the hospital.

"Could we take this to your office?" Dennis had no desire to have the conversation in front of Penny or any clients that might walk in.

"Certainly. Follow me." Troy invited them into his office and closed the door. Once seated behind his oak desk, he steepled his fingers. "So what's this all about?"

He nodded to Charlotte, and she took the lead. "I've heard that Stella and a couple of other girls may have changed their minds and decided to keep their babies."

Troy's forehead creased. "I can't say I've heard this. But it does happen from time to time."

"When it does, how do you respond?" Dennis asked.

"How else? We respect the decision and wish them well." Troy leaned back in his chair.

Charlotte stepped in again. "And the adoptive parents?"

"What about them?"

"They must not like it."

"If the girls have chosen who their baby goes to, it can be difficult on the family. But many times, we make the match. When that's the case, we typically use foster parents for two or three weeks to avoid this problem."

"Is that normal for all law offices?" Charlotte continued to question the attorney while Dennis watched him for any signs of deception.

"Not necessarily. But it's how we do things."

"What about Stella?" Charlotte asked.

"Stella? I don't recall her file."

"Excuse me?" Charlotte's brows rose to her hairline.

"Just what I said. She wasn't on my caseload."

Interesting. Dennis decided to stop questioning the man. There was something going on here, and he wanted to secure a search warrant before the lawyer got nervous and destroyed information.

He stood and held his hand out. "Thank you for seeing us, Mr. Kent."

Charlotte scowled at him, and he gave her an almost imperceptible shake of his head. She pinched her lips closed.

Troy met his gesture. "I'm not sure I helped, but you're welcome."

Dennis placed his hand on Charlotte's lower back and steered her out the door. He braced himself for the firestorm coming his way.

"What was—"

"Not here."

The office door clicked behind them, and a whoosh of cold air caused them both to secure their coats. He marched Charlotte to his SUV.

"What was that about?" The temperature outside could have risen just by the heat of Charlotte's glare.

"If you'll keep your voice down…" He scanned the parking lot. Only an old white van sat several businesses away. "I didn't want him to know who we're concerned about."

The anger that flared moments ago eased. "You're afraid if it's him, he'll cover his tracks."

He nodded.

Charlotte cringed. "Sorry."

"You had no way of knowing that I wanted to wait to get a search warrant, and I had no way of cluing you in without being obvious."

She seemed to mull over his statement. "So now what?"

"Now we go back to my place and grab a couple hours of rest, then we get back to work." He could use more than a couple of hours, but he'd take what he could get.

"Sounds good. I'll admit, I'm beat." Charlotte moved toward the passenger door and halted. Her eyes narrowed.

Dennis turned to see what had caught her attention. Nothing stood out to him, so what had caused her to stop like that? "Charlotte?"

"I thought... I'm not sure." She blew out a frustrated breath. "Never mind."

Hand on her arm, he shifted her to face him. "What did you see?"

"It's ridiculous, really."

"Let me be the judge of that."

"I thought I saw someone I knew from the past." She pointed down the parking lot. "Over there by that van."

"Who?"

"Just a guy I met at a homeless shelter years ago."

"Is it a bad thing if you did see him?" Dennis

wanted to know what he was up against if the man was violent.

"No. He was nice enough."

"Then why the hesitation?"

"I'm not sure." She stared off like her mind was searching for an answer.

"Come on. It's time to go." His gut said to get away from the attorney's office and whoever Charlotte thought she saw. And he was inclined to listen to his instincts.

NINE

Charlotte sank onto the couch after a quick lunch, laid her head back and closed her eyes. Coaching Ginny through the birth of her baby had been wonderful and heartbreaking all wrapped into one. The whole experience had left her exhausted, both physically and emotionally. Short of the house catching fire, she had no intention of getting up from her spot on the couch. Except maybe to go lie down in bed.

She reached down and buried her fingers in Theo's fur, letting the warmth soothe her battered heart. A sigh escaped. She swallowed back the tears threatening to fall and let the darkness of sleep tug her under.

Something cold and wet touching her jerked her awake. Theo nosed her hand again. She blinked and obliged his request while she forced her mind to function, only to have memories slam into her.

A little hand patted her shoulder. "Miss Charlotte."

She rolled her head and gazed into concerned gray eyes. So much like the girl's father. "Yes, Amelia?"

"Can I get you anything?"

The offer twisted her stomach. Such an adult question from a five-year-old. "No, sweetie, I'm good."

"You look sad."

When Ginny's baby was born, Charlotte had made a promise to herself. She wouldn't allow her dark thoughts to taint Amelia. The young girl had been through enough in her short life and deserved a lot more than Charlotte's bitterness.

She shifted and patted the couch. Amelia crawled next to her. She inhaled the baby shampoo the girl used and held back the sobs collecting in her throat.

Charlotte swallowed hard. "You want the truth?"

"Daddy says it's always best to tell the truth." The corners of Amelia's mouth drooped.

She brushed a wisp of hair from Amelia's face. "What do *you* think?"

The girl blew out a big breath. "I think sometimes it's hard."

"Why is that?"

Amelia shrugged.

The weight pressing on the young girl worried Charlotte. "Come on. It's just us girls. Why is it hard?"

"Because if Daddy knew the truth, he'd be mad."

Charlotte sat up straighter. Whatever the huge secret, it had Amelia tied in knots. "You know, if you tell me, maybe I can help you figure out what to do."

Amelia seemed to ponder the offer, then shifted to face her. "He's angry with my momma."

How much should she say about Amelia's situation? The girl was young but had, as they say, an *old soul*. Not to mention the kid was super smart. If Charlotte had to guess, she'd say that Amelia would hit genius level on an IQ test. Due to that and her background, she understood life better than kids twice her age. "Yes, he is. But I can understand why. She lied and kept you from him." She paused, not sure whether or not to mention the neglect.

"It's okay, Miss Charlotte. You can say it. My momma left me alone to do drugs."

Just as she suspected. The child knew more than everyone gave her credit for. "Something no child should ever experience or have to understand the meaning of."

Amelia dipped her chin to her chest. "Yeah,

well, it happened. I had to take care of myself most of the time."

She reached over and ran a hand down Amelia's hair. "Did something else happen?" The possible answers terrified Charlotte.

Amelia refused to make eye contact.

"Sweetie, what are you hiding from your daddy?"

A tear slipped down Amelia's cheek. "She'd lock me in the closet if I made her mad. Which was a lot when I was little."

Unable to stand it anymore, Charlotte pulled Amelia into her arms and held her tight. The past no longer mattered. Only the broken heart of the little girl beside her. "Is that why you started taking care of her? Cooking and cleaning?"

The little girl nodded against Charlotte's chest. "I thought maybe she'd love me then."

What did Charlotte say to that? At three and four years old, the girl in her arms had become an adult. "Amelia, I have a question for you."

The girl pulled back and peered up at her.

"Are you afraid that your dad will do the same thing?"

"No. Not really... Maybe." Pain etched Amelia's features. "He'll get mad if I tell him about the closet though."

"And what will he do?"

Amelia bit her bottom lip.

"Will he put you in a closet because he's mad?"

"No." The girl shook her head. "He wouldn't do that."

"Then what are you afraid of?" She brushed her fingers through Amelia's hair.

Big watery gray eyes stared up at her. "That he won't love me anymore."

A huge chunk of Charlotte's heart broke off and fluttered to the ground. "Honey." She cupped the girl's chin. "Your daddy loves you very much. He wants you to have a wonderful childhood. You understand that, right?"

Amelia's mouth twisted to the side.

"Sweetheart, tell me what your daddy does for you." If Amelia took a minute to see her father in a different light than her mother, maybe the girl wouldn't worry.

"He's always telling me to go play. And he cooks for me. He's told me I can tell him anything." She could almost see the wheels turning in Amelia's head. "Maybe I will tell him someday."

"Good for you. I think you'll feel better once you do."

Amelia nodded and crossed her arms. "Now quit stalling. Why are you sad?"

Charlotte almost laughed. Amelia reminded her of Theo with his favorite chew toy. "I'm remembering a little girl who's no longer with me."

"Did she die like my momma?"

"Yes, she did."

Amelia patted Charlotte's cheek. "I'm sorry."

"Me too."

"Do you miss her?"

"Every day. Do you miss your momma?"

"I guess so." Amelia snuggled in next to Charlotte. "Is it bad that I'm glad I don't live with her anymore?"

"I think that's an okay thing to feel." She draped her arm around the little girl. Odd. The vise that normally constricted her lungs hadn't tightened. "You know, it's okay to love someone and not like their actions."

Amelia tilted her head and studied Charlotte for a moment. "Really?"

"Yes. And I know your daddy loves you very much and wants the best for you."

"He doesn't like to tell me no." Mischief twinkled in the girl's eyes.

"Amelia," she playfully scolded.

"It's okay, Miss Charlotte. I won't do anything bad."

The girl was wise beyond her years. "Good. Because taking advantage of his love wouldn't be okay."

An upward curve tipped the corners of Amelia's lips. "But it's fun to tease him."

Charlotte bear-hugged the child. "Oh, girl, you are a turkey."

"I know." Amelia bounced off the couch and ruffled Theo's ears. "I have to get ready to go. My uncles are all working today, so I'm going to spend time with Miss Judith."

"Who's that?"

"The lady that lives at the old people's home."

Charlotte bit the inside of her cheek to keep from laughing.

"Bye." Amelia hurried off down the hall.

Her gaze followed the five-year-old's path. Would her daughter have been as precocious as Amelia?

She rubbed her chest to relieve the ache that never went away.

A boulder-size lump filled Dennis's throat, and his knees threatened to buckle. He grabbed the doorjamb to keep himself upright.

He'd started to leave his room after a quick nap but stopped and waited, listening to every word Amelia told Charlotte. The social worker who'd brought Amelia to him had told him about the living conditions, but he had a feeling his daughter had never revealed her mother shutting her in a closet to anyone before today.

Realization struck him like a lightning bolt. No wonder she hated to have her bedroom door closed. He'd struggled to get her to shut the bathroom door since the day she arrived on his doorstep. They'd compromised, and she used the en suite in his bedroom so that guests never walked in on her.

Once Amelia entered her bedroom, he snuck out and strode to the living room. "Thank you."

Charlotte shifted, and her gaze landed on him. "Excuse me?"

"Thank you for talking to Amelia."

Her eyes flitted to the hallway and back to him. "You were listening?"

"I didn't mean to. I almost walked in on your conversation and didn't want to intrude, so I backed out of sight." He massaged the muscles in the back of his neck. "You got her to say more in ten minutes than her therapist or I have since she came to live with me."

"I'm not sure I did anything special, but I'm glad I was able to help."

He arched a brow.

"No, seriously. I am. She's a sweet girl and, man, is she smart."

He lowered himself into the recliner and clasped his hands between his knees. "Her teacher thinks she's genius level. I'm not sure what I'm going to do in a few years when she outgrows everything I know."

Charlotte chuckled. "I don't envy you."

"Thanks a lot." He glanced toward Amelia's bedroom. "I have to drop her off with Miss Judith, who, by the way, is eighty years old but acts like she's twenty. She's kind of the town grandma. But back to the reason I came into the room. We got a lead on Hannah. A volunteer reported seeing her at a homeless shelter last night."

"Where?"

"A couple towns over in Brightwood."

Charlotte sucked in a breath. "That's a twenty-five minute drive. How did she get there?"

"I don't know, and I'm not positive it was her, but I want to check it out. I'm assuming you want to join me."

"Of course." She rose from the couch and retrieved Theo's vest. "Give me a few minutes, and we can go. I'd like to take Theo with us."

"He's welcome. Maybe he can use that amazing nose of his again." Dennis stood. "I'll go prod Amelia along so we can leave."

Thirty minutes later, with Theo happily napping in the back of the SUV, Dennis and Charlotte followed a skipping Amelia to Judith Evans's door.

His daughter knocked, and the door swung open.

"There's my girl." Judith held out her arms.

"Miss Judith!" Amelia flew into the older woman's arms and gave her a huge hug.

Dennis leaned against the door frame. "Well, I can see where I rate now."

"Oh, my dear." Judith patted his cheek. "You'll always be one of my boys, but this sweetheart—" she ran a hand over Amelia's hair "—she tops the list."

Amelia grinned at him, and he chuckled.

"Point taken." Dennis ushered Charlotte inside. "Miss Judith, I'd like you to meet Charlotte Bradley. Charlotte, this lady here is the town's gem." He kissed Judith on the temple.

"You've always been a sweet-talker, Sheriff." Judith shifted her attention to Charlotte. "Nice to meet you, young lady."

"Thank you. It's nice to meet you too." Charlotte shook Judith's hand.

"Amelia, go on into the kitchen. My no-good boyfriend, Harold, is in there eating all the snacks. You better stop him."

His daughter giggled and took off. "Bye, Daddy!"

"Bye, princess." He turned to Judith. "Thanks a ton for doing this."

"You know I'm always here for you."

And he did. Dennis hugged Judith. "You're the best."

The older woman patted his chest and studied him for a moment then turned to Charlotte.

"Honey, you're good for our sheriff. Please don't give up on him."

Charlotte's eyebrows rose to her hairline. "Miss Judith."

"Sorry, son. I just tell it like it is." She waved him away. "Now, go so I can spoil your daughter. Don't forget to lock up on your way out." Judith disappeared around the corner.

"I guess we've been dismissed." Charlotte chuckled.

"And *that* was Miss Judith." He shook his head. "Let's get to work."

With Amelia safe with Judith and her boyfriend, Harold, along with the other residents at the retirement community, Dennis and Charlotte headed out of town to investigate the lead at the homeless shelter.

He drove in silence, letting the words between Amelia and Charlotte replay in his head while he headed toward Brightwood. He glanced at Charlotte. "Do you think she's happy?"

Charlotte shifted and leaned against the passenger door. "Amelia? Yes, I do."

"Is that your professional opinion?" He tapped the steering wheel while he waited for Charlotte to answer.

"I think she's a little girl who's lived through a lot, and you are giving her the stability and love she needs to feel secure."

He blew out a breath. "Good. Good."

Charlotte bit her lower lip. "Did you know about the punishment?"

He shook his head. "No. As far as I know, she hasn't told anyone. I'm glad she confided in you."

With a shrug, Charlotte turned and looked out the passenger window. "I'm honored that she told me." After several minutes of silence, she maintained her focus on the passing scenery. "Do you think we'll find Hannah?"

"I don't know. I'm worried about her. This is the first hit we've had on her since the snowstorm."

"Do you believe in God?"

He glanced at her and back to the road. "Yes. I do."

"Would you pray for her?" She twisted the ring on her right hand.

"Of course, but you can too, you know."

She huffed. "I'm not so sure He'll listen."

Since she'd given him a glimpse into her life, he understood her hesitance about God. How did he get her to see that God was trustworthy? "He will, you know."

She returned her attention to the window. "Maybe."

The inside of the vehicle returned to the previous quiet state. Dennis let her have the moment. He wanted to know what was going on inside that mind of hers, but he refused to push. At least he'd gotten a maybe out of her.

Snow piled high in the ditches along the cleared highway. The fields and tree lines a pristine white from the snowstorm two days ago. Dennis's shoulders slumped. Had it really been less than forty-eight hours since he struggled to survive in the shallow cave?

God, I don't think I've thanked You enough for giving Charlotte the strength to save my life.

He drummed his fingers on the steering wheel. For once in his life, the silence was killing him. Time to change the subject. "Any more ideas about where you've seen that medallion?"

"No." She tapped her head. "It's like it's right here. I can visualize it but can't recall whom it belongs to. Like I said before, it could be from a TV show for all I know."

"Keep at it. Hopefully, you'll remember."

His gut screamed at him that knowing where she recognized the medallion from would blow the case wide open, but making Charlotte stress about it wouldn't help.

"Sure." She went silent again.

Theo's soft snores mixed with the SUV's heater and the hum of the tires on the pavement made Dennis wish for twelve hours of sleep. He knew Charlotte had to be exhausted, but her sudden quiet concerned him. What had sent her retreating inside herself?

A while later, he parked at the homeless shelter where Hannah might have been seen.

Dennis glanced at Charlotte and caught her nibbling on the inside of her cheek. "Something bothering you?"

She shrugged. "No, not really."

Huh, like he believed that. "All right then, ready to go in?"

With a nod, she got out and clipped Theo's leash onto his collar. "Come on, boy. Let's find Hannah."

Dennis rounded the SUV and joined Charlotte. Theo trotted next to them as they entered the building. Charlotte seemed to know where she was going, which puzzled him, but he followed her lead. When they arrived at an office marked *Director*, Dennis no longer wondered if she'd spent time volunteering at the shelter before. She had specific knowledge of the building.

With the door open, she knocked on the jamb.

A fifty-something-year-old man with tattoos peeking out from beneath his long sleeves looked up from his desk. "Charlotte Bradley. You're a sight for sore eyes."

"Hello, Mr. Parker." She stepped into the room with Theo by her side. Dennis took a spot next to her. "This is my friend, Sheriff Dennis Monroe."

The man stood and extended his hand. "Jerry Parker. Nice to meet you." After exchanging pleasantries, Mr. Parker sat down and steepled his fingers. "What can I do for you?"

Dennis pulled a picture of Hannah from his pocket and presented it to the director. "Have you seen this woman?"

Jerry took the photo, glanced at it and returned it to Dennis. "She was here last night, but I haven't seen her since."

"That was quick. Are you sure it's the same girl?" Dennis believed the man, but he had to make sure.

"Sure am." His gaze drifted to Charlotte, then to Dennis. "We don't get many pregnant women who stay here. Well, let me rephrase that. When we do get pregnant women coming in, I call Charlotte. She picks them up and takes them to Sadie's Place. A much better environment than a shelter with a transient population. We love our homeless friends, but those girls need more than we can offer."

Dennis's gaze connected with Charlotte's, and he lifted a brow.

She gave him a nod but didn't elaborate. Talk about secrets. Would she ever trust him enough to let him fully into her world? Maybe once they'd known each other for more than two days, but he had a feeling Charlotte didn't share much about herself.

"Mind if Theo takes a look around?" Charlotte patted the dog.

Jerry shook his head. "Not at all."

Dennis could tell Charlotte wanted to get moving, so he ended the impromptu meeting. "Thank you very much, Mr. Parker." He handed the man his business card. "If you see her or hear anything, please give me a call."

"Sure thing. And, Charlotte, it's good to see you again."

She forced a smile and moved into the hall. What was up with her and Jerry? Placing a hand on the small of her back, he noticed that Charlotte had brought her weapon. A fact that relaxed him a bit. He had no desire for her to use it, but having it gave her an extra layer of safety. "Where to?"

"I brought Hannah's shirt from the other day. It's still in a bag, so it should work for Theo." With a quick hand gesture, she motioned Theo to sit, then pulled the clothing item from her purse. She opened the bag and let the dog get a good whiff. "Okay, Theo, do your thing. *Find.*"

Tail and nose in the air, the dog went to work. He zigzagged through the main room and trotted into the women's sleeping quarters. Without stopping, Theo exited and headed down the back hallway to the storage area. Several praises and prompts later, he circled and whined in a dark corner of the back room.

Dennis had watched him work on the trail the other day and hadn't seen him act like this. "What's he doing?"

"He's worried." Charlotte sighed. "It's times like these I wish he could speak."

Dennis strode over to Theo, crouched beside him and held out his phone flashlight. Nothing appeared out of the ordinary. He slowly ran the light over the area again. Stuck in the corner, a hair tie lay half out and half under the baseboard. Dennis snapped a picture and collected it as though it was evidence.

He held up the small bag. "Do you think this is Hannah's?"

"The way Theo's reacting, I'd say yes." Charlotte scratched behind the dog's ears. "Good boy."

Theo growled and positioned himself between Charlotte and the doorway.

She started for her Glock.

"Don't. Leave the gun. Get behind me." Hand hovering over his weapon, Dennis stepped forward.

Charlotte obeyed his orders and slid behind him. She placed her trembling fingers on his shoulder.

"Who's there?" When no one answered, Dennis reached back and grabbed her hand. "Stay close. I think it's time to get out of here."

"I couldn't agree more."

The fur on Theo's neck remained bristled as they exited the storage room and headed for the exit. The dog hadn't liked something and still had his hackles raised as they walked through the parking lot.

Once in the SUV, Dennis processed the events. He glanced at the dog, who now had his tongue dangling out of his mouth, panting happily. What had Theo sensed in there? A scan of the area didn't upend any clues to what had set the dog off.

Charlotte lay back against the headrest. "Hannah was there. Where did she go?"

"I'd give you answers if I could, but I have no idea." Dennis grabbed his phone. "I'll check in with Kyle, but I think he would've called if they had another lead."

Before he tapped the speed dial for Kyle, Charlotte's phone rang.

"Hello." Charlotte straightened in her seat. "Ginny, I'm putting you on speaker."

"Miss B, she's gone," Ginny wailed.

"Tell me again what happened." Charlotte gave him a worried look.

"Ms. Rivers was holding Grace while I took a nap. When I woke up, they were gone."

"Did you call for the nurse? Maybe they took your daughter to give her a bath."

"No! A new nurse came in. She hasn't seen Ms. Rivers. Didn't even know she was here." A sob filled the interior of the vehicle. "Grace is gone."

"Hold on, Ginny. I'm coming. The sheriff and I will figure this out."

"Please hurry."

The line went dead.

Dennis sped from the parking lot. The SUV fishtailed when he pulled onto the main road. He rolled his hand over the top of the steering wheel and clenched his jaw. "You don't suppose the social worker stole the baby, do you?"

"I can't see it. I've known Erin for years." Charlotte's brow furrowed. "If she did, I'll be shocked."

"We can't ignore the possibility. What about her argument with Mr. Kent? It's conceivable they're in this together."

Charlotte chewed on her thumbnail. "A few days ago, I would have said no. But with all that's happened… I just don't know. And I'm the one who asked Erin to stay with Ginny. What if—"

"Don't go there, Charlotte. What's the make and model of Erin's car? I want to put a BOLO out on it just to be safe."

"A blue Ford Escape. I have no idea what

year." She swiped a hand down her face. "I don't know cars, so I'm surprised that I remember that much."

"It'll help." He placed a call to Kyle and gave him the information. His deputy promised to take care of it and contact the rest of the detectives to search. After he disconnected, he glanced over at Charlotte. Tears swam in her eyes.

With both of them lost in thought, he let the silence linger and his mind whirl with the facts.

A missing pregnant teen—Hannah. A dead teen—Stella—and her stolen baby. An attempted kidnapping—Ginny, and now her baby was missing. Along with the fact that all three girls had changed their minds about the adoptions. Oh, yeah, and he couldn't forget the attacks on Charlotte. What a mess. He rubbed his forehead. If all that didn't add up to babies being sold, he'd give up his badge.

What exactly had they stumbled upon?

TEN

Baby Grace was missing. The thought stole the air from Charlotte's lungs. She wanted to scream at Dennis to drive faster, but it wouldn't do any good. The man had flipped on the light bar and had gone twice the speed limit already.

When he slammed the SUV into Park at the hospital, she jumped out and grabbed Theo. She'd fight everyone in her way to have him with her. He might be the only one that could find Erin and the baby. Besides, she needed his comfort right now as well.

Dennis marched through the door by her side.

The receptionist rose and skirted around the desk. "I'm sorry, but you can't—"

He flashed his badge. "She's with me, and the dog stays," he said, his words more of a growl than a command.

The receptionist's mouth dropped open. "Okay, Sheriff."

Dennis took Charlotte's arm and kept her by his side. "Let's go." They made their way to the maternity ward in a matter of minutes.

Charlotte peeked in the room. "Ginny, may we come in?"

"Miss B!"

She pushed the door open and hurried to Ginny's bedside. Gathering the girl in her arms, she rocked back and forth. "Shh, we'll find her." She held the girl for several moments then eased back. "I brought Theo. We can try to track Grace down, assuming I can find something she wore or held close."

"I don't have anything." Ginny pointed to the floor under the chair. "But that's the blanket the nurse gave Ms. Rivers to keep warm while she stayed with me."

"That should work for Erin at least." She hoped baby Grace was with the social worker, and they'd find them both in the hospital. Charlotte found a plastic bag in the drawer of the end table and gathered the cloth. "I hate to leave you, but if we don't get moving, our window of opportunity to find her might fade."

"Go." Ginny wiped her eyes. "Please bring my baby back."

Dennis stepped forward. "I promise that we'll do our very best. I have a dozen deputies out there looking for her right this very minute."

Tears streamed down Ginny's cheeks. "Thank you."

He turned to Charlotte. "Let's get moving."

She nodded and guided Theo to the hall, where she opened the bag and gave the dog a good sniff. "*Find.*"

Theo lifted his nose and took off toward the stairwell.

The relief that he'd found Erin's scent was palpable. She jogged to keep up and followed Theo down the stairs to a janitor's closet. He sniffed the air and bolted out the exit.

Dennis joined her as she ran after Theo. "He's got something."

"I hope it's enough." For the first time in years, Charlotte wanted to pray. Would God listen to her pleas unlike the last time? It didn't matter if there was the slimmest of possibilities—she had to try.

God, please help us find Erin and the baby. Don't let any harm come to either of them.

No sooner than she thought the words, Dennis's phone rang.

"Sheriff Monroe." His gaze met hers. "Where?" Another pause. "On my way."

"What is it?"

"They found Erin's car crashed in a ditch."

"Is she okay? Was the baby with her?"

"Charlotte, the car is empty...except for an infant carrier."

A whimper escaped her lips, and her legs turned to jelly. "Oh, please, no." Strong arms circled her waist and held her upright.

Her friend just couldn't be responsible for stealing babies.

After a moment, Dennis released her. "Ready?"

"Theo, *come*." Her girls needed her. She refused to fall apart. Putting more strength in her steps than she possessed, Charlotte strode next to Dennis around the building to his SUV.

He opened the rear passenger door for Theo, then Dennis moved to her door and assisted her in. Always the gentleman in more ways than one. He slipped behind the wheel, turned on his light bar and headed to the crime scene while she gathered her composure. Whatever awaited deserved her full attention.

"According to Kyle, there's no blood or signs of injury in the baby seat. However, the driver hit their head on the side window. At least we can get DNA from that."

"A fat lot of good that will do if the baby vanishes," she snapped.

He glanced at her, and his brows rose to his hairline.

"Sorry. I'm…" She was what? Frustrated. Furious. In over her head. She exhaled. Honestly, all the above. "How quick can you get the results back?"

"You're right, it'll take too long. However, if we find someone with a cut on the side of their head, we have a possible suspect." He forced a smile.

"Then let's hope we find who we're looking for."

Several minutes later, Dennis pulled in behind another sheriff's department vehicle.

"Let's leave Theo in the SUV for a bit. I want to get a look at the car and make a plan."

Charlotte nodded and slipped from the passenger's seat. She leaned in and patted Theo's head. "Be a good boy. I'll be back soon." She latched the door closed and joined Dennis.

A frigid wind whipped along the edge of the road and snuck under her collar. The temps had started to drop again. With Hannah still missing, and now Ginny's baby gone too, her anxiety ratcheted up several notches. She snuggled deeper into her coat and plodded along with Dennis to the wrecked car.

"Is that Ms. Rivers's sedan?" Dennis asked.

A deep gash cut through her heart. Her friend couldn't be involved, but the evidence suggested differently. "Yes. That's hers."

"Hey, Sheriff." Jason shoved his gloved hands into the pockets of his department jacket and bounced on his toes. "What do you say we solve this mystery so we can enjoy a nice fireplace?"

The nonchalant attitude irked Charlotte, but she refrained from voicing her opinion. She understood the easy comment, but with her girls in the center of whatever was happening, Charlotte's patience and tolerance were limited. But still, Jason was one of the good guys.

Dennis shook his head at his deputy. "What have you found?"

"Car's empty. But like I told you over the phone, there's a car seat in the back and blood on the driver's side window."

"Only one adult in the car?"

"From what I can tell. However, I took a guess and printed the passenger side."

"And?"

"There's a handprint like someone braced themselves, but it might not mean anything."

Charlotte blew out a breath and watched as white swirled from her lips. "I don't understand."

Dennis shifted his gaze to her. "Meaning, it could have been left from another time and not today."

"Oh." Her hope deflated like someone had poked a needle in a balloon.

"Jason, can you stay here with Charlotte please?"

"Sure thing, boss." Jason sidled up close to her and made a constant scan of the surroundings.

Apparently, she now had a bodyguard.

In full sheriff mode, Dennis examined the scene from all angles. He threw a couple of questions at Jason and snapped pictures with his phone. Once finished, he rejoined her. "There seem to be footprints in the snow, but this wind is messing up the tracks. I'm not sure which way to start searching."

"Theo can do it."

"In this wind?"

She thought for a minute. Theo was an air-scent dog, and the breeze would make it difficult, if not impossible, but she had to try. Especially with a baby's life at stake. "He's one of the best." She spun and marched to the SUV and released her dog.

"You have a lot of faith in his abilities." Dennis joined her and snagged an industrial flashlight and his radio from the vehicle.

She gathered her small waist pack that held Theo's things. "What choice do we have?"

"You've got a point." He jerked his head toward the wrecked car. "Come on."

The last winter storm had dumped several feet of snow, and the weather forecaster, not to mention the freezing temps, warned of more on the way. They had to find Ginny's baby and fast.

"I need a scent of the baby for Theo to work with."

Jason's lips pursed then his eyes widened. "I'll take the cover off the car seat. Will that work?"

"It'll have to."

The deputy gathered the cover and handed it to Dennis. "One car seat thingy."

Dennis rolled his eyes. "Thanks. Now take whatever photos you need, get a tow truck out here and get out of the cold before Mel blames me that you're sick."

Jason gave him a mock salute and hurried about his business.

"Let's see what that dog of yours can do."

Charlotte slipped on Theo's vest and attached his leash. "All right, boy." She let him get a big whiff of the scent. "*Find.*"

Theo's nose went in the air. He wove back and forth a couple of times, then ran toward the woods on the other side of the road. After a few zigzags, he stood and sniffed the air.

She took pity on the dog and gave him the scent again. "*Find again.*"

The wind blew Theo's fur back, and he closed his eyes against the swirling snow. He suddenly straightened and took off, running in the opposite direction.

"I think he's confused." Dennis jogged next to her.

"Trust him. He knows what he's doing." *God, now would be a good time to prove me wrong about You not listening.* Her lungs burned, and tears trickled down her cheeks from the cold air.

Theo darted through the trees. His paws crunched on the frozen ground. She silently scolded herself for not putting on his booties. His health and safety were everything, and she'd blown it. However, Theo didn't appear to care.

She and Dennis struggled to keep up, but the dog was on to something.

"Okay, so I was wrong. He knows where he's going." Dennis's breathy admission surprised her.

The snarky words *ya think* sat on her lips, but she refrained from letting them loose.

"What? You aren't going to rub it in?" His teasing tone had a smile curving on her lips.

"I'll be nice." At the last moment, she noticed a low-hanging branch and ducked under it just in time, saving herself from a nice scratch on her face.

A signal bark filled the air.

"Theo's found the baby." Excitement mixed with dread stirred in her belly. Was the baby dead or alive?

"Come on." Dennis grabbed her hand, and together they ran toward the dog.

An open area among the trees lay before them. Theo sat in the middle and barked again.

Dennis spun in a circle. "Where?"

She had no idea, but she trusted her dog. Glancing at Theo then in the direction he faced, Charlotte narrowed her gaze. Her breath caught. The edge of a baby blanket stuck out beneath a section of brush. "There."

Dennis sprinted the short distance to the tangle of dead tree limbs covered in snow. He hefted the branches, tossed them aside and dropped to his knees.

Charlotte stood back, unsure if she wanted the answer to what lay out of sight. She patted Theo's head. "Good boy."

"Charlotte." Dennis motioned her to join him.

"Theo, *stay*." Inching forward, she wrapped her arms around her middle the best she could with her coat in the way. "W-what did you find?"

"It's not the baby. There's someone here, but the little girl isn't anywhere to be found."

Her stomach that threatened to revolt settled a bit. "Theo alerted to the blanket like he did to Hannah's scarf." She made her way to his side and looked down. Dennis wiped snow from a woman's face. The limp form stared with lifeless eyes toward the sky. "It's not Erin."

"Do you recognize her?"

Her mind spun and refused to focus. Where was the baby? And what about Erin? Did her friend take the infant? She forced the circling questions from her brain and thought for a moment. She shook her head. "No... Wait. That's the nurse Ginny had during delivery."

"Are you sure?"

"Positive. I probably wouldn't have noticed, but it triggered a memory. She reminded me of the nurse who coached me when I had my baby. The similarities were uncanny." Charlotte tilted her head and studied the woman whose life had ended too soon.

"Is it the same woman? I mean, that helped both of you?"

She shrugged. "I remember the nurse because she stayed by my side when I had no one. It's been five years. Maybe the past has blurred my memory, but I doubt it."

"Keep thinking about it. Don't make assumptions."

His words sent a shiver up her spine. "What are you thinking?"

"Nothing specific. Just that I don't want to miss any possibility no matter how improbable."

A gust of wind had her jamming her gloved hands farther into her pockets. "How did she die?"

"She has a gash on her temple that matches hitting her head on the car window."

"So she was the driver."

He nodded. "That would be my guess. But that's not what killed her. I'm guessing the strangulation marks on her throat have something to do with her death. However, I'm leaving the cause of death to Melanie, or she might do bodily damage to *me* if I misspeak." Dennis pulled out his phone and placed the call to the coroner's office. "They'll be here soon."

Ice crackled in the distance.

Dennis shot to his feet and yanked the gun from his holster.

The queasiness of finding a dead woman switched to the cold sweat of being hunted. The eerie feeling struck her like a two-by-four between the eyes. "Dennis." Her voice quivered.

"I don't like this. We're too out in the open. Call Theo and follow me."

Without hesitation, she complied. "Theo, *come.*" The dog bounded over, and she clipped on his leash and hurried alongside Dennis. "Where to?"

"The woods. You'll be hidden, and I'll still be able to see the crime scene." He gripped her forearm and yanked her behind a large tree.

Charlotte pressed her back against the trunk. Dennis stood inches from her, peering over her shoulder. His breath tickled her cheek.

"See anything?"

"No."

Theo took up a protective stance next to her leg, ready to defend.

The intensity of Dennis's response squeezed the air from her lungs.

So…she hadn't imagined the danger.

Snow swirled off the ground and into Dennis's eyes, sticking to his lashes. The wind had kicked up a notch, and the temperatures had dropped several degrees since he and Charlotte left the hospital. His body hummed with adrenaline. Was the attacker out there, or had paranoia wrapped its icy fingers around him?

The crackle of hardened snow joined the whistle of the breeze through the trees. He held his weapon at the ready and peered around the large trunk. His lungs deflated when he spotted Kyle striding toward the body.

"Kyle's arrived. Let's go have a chat with him and get you out of here." He stepped back, giving her room to breathe.

Her teeth scraped her lower lip. "Are you sure it's safe?"

"Honestly, not really, but the sooner we hand things over to Kyle, the faster we can leave." He tucked Charlotte in next to him and plodded to the crime scene.

Mouth open to give his rundown of information, Dennis lasered in on Kyle's grief-stricken gaze and paused. The man stood staring at the woman's body. Dennis knew the problem but had no comforting words for his deputy.

He released Charlotte and joined Kyle. He placed a hand on his deputy's shoulder. "It's not her, man."

"I know. But the hair." Kyle swallowed hard.

Deputy Howard's fiancée had died in the line of duty last month. The entire Anderson County Sheriff's Department had rallied around him, but the death had rocked his deputy to the core. Kyle had come back to work a couple of weeks ago, but Dennis had avoided giving him homicides, except for collecting evidence after the coroner had removed the body. He hadn't intended for Kyle to take this one, but sometimes he had no choice.

"Are you going to be okay with this scene?"

Kyle straightened his shoulders. "I have to be. I have a job to do."

Not exactly what Dennis meant, but he trusted his men and women to be truthful, so he'd take Kyle at his word. "Then we'll leave you to it." He turned to Charlotte. "Ready?"

Charlotte froze. Head tilted, she stared at the dead woman. Bewilderment flickered in her eyes, twisting his gut.

Instinct told him to comfort her, but his brain kicked in, and he waited her out.

"I know her."

Now it was his turn to be confused. "We already decided that. She's Ginny's nurse."

"No. That's not it." She crouched and narrowed her gaze on the woman.

Dennis moved closer. "What is it?"

"Kyle, would you roll her arm a little so I can see the inside of her wrist."

The deputy removed his winter gloves, replaced them with a pair of nitrile ones and gave Charlotte the view she asked for.

She gasped and awkwardly staggered backward.

Dennis grabbed her arm, pulled her to a standing position and steadied her.

"The rose. She… It's… Oh, my." Charlotte's hand flew to her mouth.

Kyle rested the woman's arm on the ground and stood.

Dennis didn't have an answer for the question in Kyle's eyes. He reached out and clasped Charlotte's hand. "What about the rose tattoo?"

She spun and buried her face in his chest. Her body shook in his arms.

The need to comfort warred with the necessity of moving Charlotte to a more secure location. "Talk to me. What has you rattled?"

"It *is* the same nurse. My nurse from five years ago." Her muffled words sent shock waves through him.

His gaze darted from the dead woman to Charlotte and back. "Are you positive?"

"That rose was my focus point during labor. I don't know why I didn't remember it earlier." She leaned back. "What does all this mean?"

Kyle folded his arms. "It means that you're tied to this woman, and we need to figure out why."

With everything in him, Dennis wanted to disagree, but he didn't believe in coincidences. And this was a big one that his mind refused to accept. "Kyle, tell Melanie to get here A-SAP. I'm taking Charlotte and getting out of here."

"On it. I'll catch up with you later at your place." Kyle withdrew the camera from the bag he'd brought and started snapping pictures.

While his deputy worked, Dennis guided Charlotte to the road, Theo on one side and Dennis on the other. He waved at Jason, who stood talking to the tow truck driver, and opened the SUV doors for her and the dog. Once inside and secure, he skirted to the front of the vehicle and climbed behind the steering wheel.

"Now what?" Theo rested his snout on Charlotte's shoulder, and she scratched his nose.

"I'd like to take you and your buddy to the station so I can grab the files and evidence. Then we can lay it all out again and see if we can find something that unravels the case."

"We can do that. Assuming the boss doesn't

mind a dog in the office." She glanced at him and forced a smile.

"I don't know. He's been a grouch lately. You'll have to ask nicely." He lay his hand on hers and squeezed her fingers.

"I still don't understand… Why me?"

"That's what I intend to find out." Days like today, he struggled with his single-father status. His daughter needed him, but the investigation required his attention. How did other single parents do it?

He rubbed the stubble on his jaw and made a mental to-do list. Call Judith and ask if she'd keep Amelia. If she couldn't, he'd call Amy. Even though he hated to bother her, he would if he had to. Next, compile all the evidence, box it up, sign the chain of evidence log and take it to his house. Finally, he'd call the judge and see if she'd approved the warrant for Troy Kent and Associates' files pertaining to any adoptions related to teens from Sadie's Place. He'd like to see all the adoption files but knew no judge would agree to that. He'd take what he could get.

He flipped a U-turn and headed toward town. The sun had lowered and sat on the horizon, waiting another hour before disappearing out of sight. The calming hues of purple, red and orange that painted the sky had no effect on him tonight. Tension had gripped him and dug into his skin. They had to find the missing babies and teen before anyone else ended up dead.

"Dennis."

"Hmm?"

"Thank you."

His gaze shifted to her, then back to the road. "What for?"

"Oh, I don't know. Putting up with me. Getting shot at. Giving up time with your daughter. You know…" She shrugged. "Everything."

How did he respond to that? He *had* sacrificed his personal life, but there was something about Charlotte that made him want to comfort and protect her. Which was ridiculous since she struggled with his daughter. But he now understood, and she was trying. A thought that made him a bit too happy.

He decided on a simple response. "You're welcome."

Twenty minutes later, he pulled into the station parking lot and cut the engine. "Once we're inside, I'll get you and Theo settled in the conference room, then I have a couple of phone calls to make."

"Whatever you need. I just want to find Hannah and the two missing babies. I'm really worried about all of them."

"Me too." He escorted her into the building and to the conference room. "There's a couch and coffee bar. You can warm up with a hot cup of coffee and take a catnap if you'd like. Although Brenda will be bringing in the boxes and files, so the nap might be iffy. I'll be back soon."

She slipped past him and entered the room. "I'll start with the coffee and go from there." She eyed the couch. "Maybe."

He chuckled. "Lie down, Charlotte. As soon as I'm finished gathering the information, and we get to my house, there won't be time to rest."

"The couch it is."

After she reclined on the couch and closed her eyes, Theo curled on the floor next to her. The woman was exhausted, and he was envious of her opportunity to rest.

He rubbed the grit from his eyes, quietly closed the door and strode to the main office. "Brenda."

His administrative assistant held up a finger, asking him to wait while she finished typing something on the computer.

Dennis sat on the edge of her desk and grabbed a rubber band lying next to her planner. He stretched it and rolled it with his fingers while he waited.

The clicking stopped, and she looked up at him. "Yes, sir?"

"I need all the evidence from the current missing person's case and the baby abduction. I'll be in my office if you need me." He turned and strode to his personal space without waiting for a response.

"Sure thing, *boss*," Brenda called after him with more than a touch of sarcasm.

He had to smile at his new assistant. Soon after he'd hired her several months ago, he'd thought he made a huge mistake. But the longer they worked together, the more he appreciated her abilities and her personality. She definitely kept him on his toes. He closed the door behind him and plopped into his chair. It seemed like weeks since he'd sat behind his desk, pushing papers.

With a sigh, he picked up his phone and placed his first call. He tapped his pen on the desk pad as the phone rang. The world had never felt quite so heavy as it did right now.

He arranged for Judith to keep Amelia, then called Doug. The missing social worker had Dennis scratching his head. Was she involved, or was she another victim?

The call connected, and Doug answered.

Dennis tossed his pen onto the desk. "Any word on Erin Rivers?"

"Not yet. I've interviewed everyone at the hospital. They recall seeing her with Ginny's baby, but no one saw her leave."

"Keep on it. She didn't vanish."

"Will do."

Dennis lowered his head into his hands and

closed his eyes. He needed to catch a break in the case before things got worse. Exhaling, he continued with his calls.

After talking to the judge, he dialed Keith's number.

"Young."

"Keith, the judge gave us the warrant."

"Thank You, God."

"Amen to that. I'd like you to grab it and head to Mr. Kent's office. Get copies of everything on the warrant and bring it to my house."

"I take it we're having one of our famous brainstorming sessions."

"I'm not sure I'd call them famous, but yes. However, I'll understand if you want to bow out. You haven't had much time with Amy and Carter lately."

"I'll be there. Amy understands, and Carter and I are just fine. But I might take you up on some time off once we get this creep."

Dennis had to smile. His deputies—his friends—always came through for each other. "And I *might* grant it."

"See you in a few." Keith chuckled and disconnected the call.

The door opened a crack, and Brenda stuck her head in. "Boxes and files are ready to go. Hand me your keys, and I'll load your SUV."

He dug the keys out of his pocket and tossed

them to her. "Brenda, I take back every bad thing I've ever said about you."

She laughed. "No, you don't, but nice try." With that, she was gone.

Time to collect Charlotte and Theo and put an end to all this.

He had to find Hannah and Ginny's baby, not to mention Stella's newborn, before it was too late.

ELEVEN

Jokes and jabs filled the air along with the shuffling of papers and clank of Pepsi and Root Beer cans on the dining room table. Charlotte struggled to keep up with the conversations. Her mind refused to let go of the worry for her girls, making concentrating difficult. She'd released Theo to roam the backyard, but temptation pushed her to bring him inside for moral support.

An elbow nudged her, and she glanced up into Dennis's compassionate gray eyes. "Here." He handed her a cup of hot chocolate. "I figured you could use the warmth, and Mel and Amy have schooled me that chocolate solves a multitude of problems."

She accepted the mug. Her fingers brushed his, sending the butterflies loose in her belly again. "Mel and Amy are smart women."

"Yes, they are." He smiled, then leaned down and whispered, "But don't tell them I said that."

The one thing about the local sheriff, he sure knew how to settle her nerves. She watched him slip onto the chair next to her and help organize the files on the table. The man was good—really good—at his job. He knew when to add a well-placed suggestion or give encouragement to his deputies. Just by being around the group for the past couple of days, she'd seen, for lack of better words, their willingness to follow him into battle without an explanation.

"All right, folks, it's late. Let's get down to business. I'd like to sleep sometime in the next week." He rubbed his eyes with his thumb and forefinger. "Anyone heard from Keith?"

The front door slammed shut. "Keith is here bearing loads of documents." Detective Keith Young waltzed into the dining room, hefting a file box. "Where do you want it?"

"Over here next to your wife." Kyle pointed to the floor beside Amy. "We pulled the coffee table in from the living room to give us an additional flat surface."

Keith placed the box on the ground, gave Amy a quick kiss and lifted the lid. "Mr. Kent wasn't exactly happy to give up his case files, but his wife and his administrative assistant, Penny, pulled everything together for me."

"They were both there?" Charlotte sipped her

hot chocolate. "I thought they worked different hours."

"I think they do. But wifey came in to talk to Kent." Keith shrugged. "Oh yeah, the guy from their cleaning service walked in while they were making copies, and Mr. Kent finished up a meeting with a Mr. Parker. It was a regular party."

Dennis scrunched his forehead. "Why on earth was their custodian there?"

Keith raised a brow and tapped his watch. "After hours, man."

"You have a point." He shifted to Charlotte. "You don't think it's the same Mr. Parker from the homeless shelter, do you?"

"I don't know why he'd be there, but I guess it's possible. I mean, how many Mr. Parkers live in the area?" Mr. Parker had helped her during the most desperate time in her life. He'd led her to a home similar to Sadie's Place in the next county over that gave her somewhere safe to live and the support she needed during her pregnancy.

"Could he be involved in all this?"

"My heart says no, but my head knows that just because I don't want to believe it, doesn't mean it's not true."

Dennis pinched his lips and turned to the others. "Put him on the list of possible suspects."

"At this point, we should add anyone whose

name pops up." Amy reached across Keith and grabbed another file.

Keith tapped her nose and smiled. "One long list coming up."

"Ugh. Give it a rest, you two." Jason pretended to gag.

Dennis laughed. "You're one to talk."

Pain flickered on Kyle's face, and his Adam's apple bobbed. "If you all are finished, you think we can get back to work?"

Dennis nodded at his deputy. "Sorry. You're right. Doug, grab that big whiteboard and prop it on a couple of chairs."

"Sure thing."

After Doug took care of the task, the rest of the group threw out names of anyone involved.

Melanie stood, arched her back and wandered to the board. "All right, everyone. We have three girls that we know of. Hannah, who is still missing. Stella, who is dead, and her baby is missing. And Ginny, who is at the hospital, but her baby is missing."

"Yes. If our theory of an illegal adoption ring is right, there might be others, but I think we should focus on these three," Charlotte added. "If we dig deeper and find more, we'll get too bogged down."

"I agree, for now. We'll increase the parameters if we need to," Melanie said.

Jason joined his wife. "So we have Mr. Kent,

his wife, Donna, and his admin, Penny. Our dead nurse—"

"Carol Adams." Everyone looked at Kyle. The corner of his mouth tilted upward. "I called the hospital."

"What Kyle said. Our dead nurse is Carol Adams."

Dennis shifted to face Doug. "Any word on our social worker Erin Rivers?"

"Not yet. It's weird. It's like she just up and disappeared."

"That doesn't sound good." The idea of Erin's involvement didn't sit well with Charlotte. She trusted Erin. Had worked with her for a long time. No, Charlotte refused to believe it. "I'm still in the camp of something happened to her."

Doug shrugged. "It's anyone's guess. But I saw the preliminary report. Someone killed the nurse and took that baby. So, another person was there. The question of the night is whether or not it was Erin Rivers."

"Who do we have searching for Erin?" Dennis asked.

"Tara's on it. She'll call if she discovers anything." Doug took a sip of his Pepsi and sat it on the table.

"What else do we have? Anyone check on the other hospital staff?" Dennis grabbed a pad of paper and scribbled notes.

Jason crossed his arms and leaned against the wall next to where the whiteboard sat. "Deputy Lewis is watching over Ginny, but he has his laptop and is running background checks on all the employees. Nothing's come up yet."

Dennis sighed. "All right. Anything we aren't covering?"

The team shook their heads.

Charlotte's hope dwindled. She stood and placed a hand on Dennis's shoulder. "It's late. I'm going to let Theo in. Be right back." She ambled to the back door and slid it open. The security light clicked on when she stepped onto the covered back porch. She looked out into the fenced-in backyard and spotted her dog chasing dried leaves across the ground. What a silly guy. "Theo, *come.*"

The dog bounded over and sat at her feet. His pink tongue hung out as he panted.

"You're such a good boy." She scratched his head. "Did you enjoy your outside time?" Charlotte received a lick on her hand in response. She chuckled. "I'll take that as a yes."

Darkness had descended, and the moon glowed a soft white against the black background sprinkled with white dots. The cold sneaked under her sweater, causing her to shiver, but the crisp air and the slight rustle of the trees gave her a moment of peace from all the crazy.

God, are You really listening?

She waited for an answer but didn't get one. Not even a twinge in her heart. Had He really abandoned her five years ago, or had she walked away from Him? With the future of too many babies and women depending on what happened next, she owed it to her girls and her friend Erin to put the pain of the past aside and go to the only one who had the ability to influence the outcome.

Charlotte sighed. *God. I'm sorry I quit trusting You. But it really hurt to lose Kayley. I don't want my girls to know that pain. Please let Erin be okay. Don't let her be involved. Thank You for placing Dennis in my life. He's an amazing man.* She inhaled the crisp air and stared into the night.

An arm draped over her shoulders and pulled her in close.

She glanced up into Dennis's gray eyes. "Did you give up in there?"

"Never. But you were out here longer than I thought you'd be. I came to check on you."

"Just putting my heart back in order."

He tilted his head. "Come again?"

"Having a chat with God."

"Oh. Oh!" He tightened his hold. "That's a good thing."

"Yes. It is." And it was. A calm had enveloped her, and hope returned.

Dennis turned her to face him and placed his

hands on the sides of her face. "I don't think I've told you how much I've come to enjoy your company."

"My company, huh?"

His eyes searched hers. "Charlotte, I'm not sure when it happened, but you've stirred feelings in me that I thought I'd never experience again."

She smirked. "Go on."

He opened his mouth, closed it, then laughed. "Okay, I take it back."

"No way. No take backs." She wrapped her arms around him. "I can't thank you enough for everything you've done. Including helping me see that I can move beyond my past. And if you haven't noticed, Sheriff, I like you too."

"I'd hoped."

"Good." She stayed in the cocoon of his embrace for several minutes. As much as she wanted to remain in his arms, she forced herself to step away. "We should go in and help."

"What if I don't want to?"

She hooked her arm around his elbow. "Come on, boss man. You have work to do." The weight of the situation came crashing down, and she sucked in a breath.

"Charlotte?" With his finger under her chin, he lifted her gaze to meet his. "Tell me what's wrong."

"Sorry. I feel guilty for enjoying myself, even for a moment."

"You have to pace yourself. A little levity and time to relax is a must, or you'll burn out. Sometimes cases take time. You can't go nonstop. No one can. Why do you think the guys in there joke around so much?"

When Charlotte didn't respond, he continued, "It's not that they disrespect the victims or families. Far from it. But they'd crack under the pressure if they don't let it go for a bit."

His words soaked in and eased her concern. "You're right." She snapped her fingers. "Come on, Theo. It's bedtime for you."

The dog ambled over and huffed, making her chuckle.

"Let's see if we can put a few more pieces together before we all fall asleep sitting upright."

"Sounds like a plan." Charlotte slid open the door and walked inside. Dennis followed and refilled the snacks while she put Theo to bed.

She glanced at the clock. Midnight. And they were no closer to finding the missing than they were hours ago. Time for her to steel herself for a long night.

During the night, everyone took turns getting an hour or two of shut-eye then returned to the information search.

At eight in the morning, with bleary eyes and

rumpled clothes, they continued to toss out ideas, cross off suspects, and add new ones. The group looked as though they'd been dragged behind a truck, and yet they hadn't found a solid lead. Not to mention, Erin was still missing. Doug had left hours ago to continue the search for Charlotte's friend.

Charlotte wanted to cry from the exhaustion and lack of progress. She'd let Theo out to roam in the backyard a little while ago, but now wished he was by her side.

"Who has the birth and death records?" Dennis rubbed the back of his neck and exhaled.

Kyle waved a paper in the air. "I do."

"Run it down for us."

Kyle flipped through the pages of records from the surrounding hospitals. "In the last five years, I've found twenty-three names that match Troy Kent's clients. Out of those, eight have infant death records."

Jason whistled. "That's a thirty-five percent death rate. Something fishy's going on."

"I think you're right." Dennis leaned forward, placed his elbows on the table and folded his hands. "What do the death certificates say? Were there any autopsies done?"

Melanie studied the files. "Well, that's odd."

Charlotte put down the pad of paper she'd kept notes on. "What?"

"No autopsies. But the weird thing is that all eight were signed by a Dr. Simmons."

"Wait. Eight deaths, three different hospitals and the same doctor on the death certificates?" Kyle sat up straight and shook his head. "Statistically, what are the odds of that happening?"

Charlotte let the numbers sink in. The hospital she gave birth in was on their list. Her stomach twisted. "Are you trying to say that those babies didn't die but were taken?"

Dennis gripped her hand and squeezed. "I'd say it's a possibility."

"You mean my Kayley might…" She couldn't finish the thought. Five years of mourning her infant, and her daughter might be alive? Tears burned but didn't fall. She refused to hope. What good would it do her? Even if Kayley were alive, Charlotte had no idea where to find her baby girl. Correction. Her five-year-old daughter.

"Don't, Charlotte. Not yet." Dennis rubbed her back. "Let's find who's responsible, then we'll tackle that mystery."

"You're right. We have to find Ginny's and Stella's babies. And Hannah, before it's too late."

She looked up to see questioning glances from the men and woman around her, but thankfully they didn't ask.

Heads down for the next forty minutes, the group searched the documents and made notes on the board. Charlotte appreciated the intensity with which these people approached the investigation. Dennis had shown her kindness and comfort over the long night, and her heart had fallen more and more for the man next to her.

"Dennis." Kyle's serious tone had Charlotte pausing her search.

"What's up?" Dennis shifted his attention to his deputy.

"Take a look." Kyle handed Dennis the document. "This is a list of twenty-three teenage women who gave birth."

"And?"

"None of them list a name on the father line."

"None?" Dennis studied the paper. "It would make it easy to take the baby. No boyfriend to come ask questions, and the girls would be in no condition to put up a fight at that point. Plus, if the girls' parents weren't in the picture…"

Charlotte knew the pain of being scared and alone. "I know my baby's father wasn't in the picture. And since—"

"Charlotte." The hard edge of Dennis's voice startled her. "You didn't tell the father about your baby?"

"I—"

"Don't you think he deserved to know? You should have told him." Red crept up his neck and onto his face.

He couldn't be serious. But one look into his eyes told her the man had judged her and found her guilty. Her heart rate skyrocketed, and fury simmered beneath the surface, ready to explode.

"How dare you! You have no idea what you're talking about."

"Don't I?" His clenched jaw twitched. "You decided to keep the father in the dark."

She pushed back and stood, knocking over her chair. "Not every woman is like Tina."

"You did the same thing! What am I supposed to think?"

Where had the easygoing, sensitive man she'd come to know gone? Not once had Dennis raised his voice around her. But here he was blaming her for something he had no knowledge of.

For once, she'd thought she'd found someone who'd support her. Believe in her. And treasure her. But no. Dennis wasn't any different than the others she'd grown up around.

"Well, since you have it all figured out, I guess I'd be wasting my time responding."

The ache in her heart—almost unbearable. She had to get some air before she fell apart. Charlotte stomped to the entry, grabbed her keys and spun around. She couldn't take it anymore.

"For your information, Kayley's father wanted nothing to do with me or his child. He told me to get rid of her and said that I had gotten pregnant on purpose. That I'd tried to trap him into marrying him."

The room had grown silent.

"I guess you're just like he was. Blaming me for something I didn't do. So, Mr. High and Mighty, you shouldn't accuse people before you have all the facts!"

The group sat, eyes wide at her outburst, but she didn't care. She stormed out the front door without her coat and hurried to her SUV.

Hands on the side of the vehicle, she bowed her head. *God, why did he have to turn out to be a jerk? I thought, maybe, just maybe, Dennis was the one.*

Her cell phone pinged with a text message. She dug it out of her pocket and glanced at the screen. Her breath caught as she read Hannah's message.

I need help.

Charlotte hurried to respond.

What happened?

No response came. She prayed the teen was all right.

She stuffed the phone into her pants pocket and looked at the house. What choice did she have? She might be mad, but she wasn't stupid. She had to tell Dennis about the message.

A hand covered her mouth, and something sharp pricked her neck. She opened her mouth to scream, but nothing came out.

Tears filled her eyes as the world dimmed.

She had no one to blame but herself. Her carelessness had caused her demise.

Dennis rubbed his tired eyes and forced down his anger. Would Tina's betrayal always follow him?

"Dude, what got into you? That was all kinds of wrong." Kyle's bluntness was like a slap to the face.

He ran a hand across the back of his neck. He'd always prided himself on the calm way he handled life. But yeah, he got it. "Not my most glowing moment."

"No argument here." His deputy wasn't cutting him any slack.

"Dennis." He shifted his gaze to Amy. "You're exhausted and aren't thinking straight. We all understand why you'd jump to those conclusions, but I think you need to go to Charlotte. Talk to her."

Keith laced his fingers with Amy's. "We learned the hard way that not everything is what it seems."

"I get that. I really do. But you all know Amelia's story. If I had known about my daughter, I wouldn't have missed out on five years of her life. And she wouldn't have endured an abusive home." Tension crept up his neck. It was a good thing no one was taking his blood pressure, because it would be through the roof. He inhaled a lungful of air and blew it out through pursed lips. "Charlotte couldn't have told the baby's father."

"Are you sure about that?" Jason challenged.

"Do you see his name on that birth certificate?"

"That's not what I asked." Jason pointed to the screen. "How do you know she's lying and didn't tell him?"

"What father in his right mind wouldn't want his baby?"

Kyle stood and placed a hand on Dennis's shoulder. "You're an awesome boss, and I'm happy to call you a friend, but you seriously need to consider what you just said." After a tight squeeze of his hand, Kyle walked into the kitchen.

His friends were right. Not all men were trustworthy, and not all women were honest. But deep down, he knew Charlotte hadn't lied. He should have asked, not accused her. Wow, he'd really messed up.

An engine rumbled, and Theo's barking intensified.

"You don't think Charlotte took off, do you? And what's going on with that dog?" Dennis debated which direction to go first. "I'll check on Charlotte." He called to Kyle since he was closest to the back door, "Kyle, will you check on Theo?"

"Sure." The slider brushed open, then closed with a smack.

Dennis hurried out the front door and stopped in his tracks. Charlotte's SUV sat under the tree, but her purse lay on the ground, its contents spread over the driveway. "Charlotte!"

The lack of response sent his heart racing. He ran to the items and spun in a circle. Charlotte was nowhere to be seen.

Where was she?

He searched the surrounding area for a few minutes and rushed back to the porch. "Hey, guys!"

His friends burst through the door.

"She's gone." His chest heaved as he tried to catch his breath, which had nothing to do with exertion.

Kyle appeared from around the corner with the dog on his heels. "Theo here was about to jump the fence."

"He knew something was wrong." Dennis ran his fingers through his hair. "Where is she?"

Jason crouched next to Charlotte's belongings. "I know I'm stating the obvious, but it looks like someone took her."

"But why take her and not just kill her?" Kyle joined Jason next to the scattered items.

"Thanks a lot." Dennis wanted to clock his deputy for the blunt comment, but Kyle had a point. "You're right. After all the attempts on her life, why change and take her?"

"It doesn't make sense." Jason stood. "But the good thing is she's still alive."

Dennis's shoulders sagged. "We hope."

"I'll hit the road and see what I can find. You guys stay here and see if you can figure out who took her." Jason jogged to his truck. "I'll get the other deputies to be on the lookout as well. I'll call you when I know something." He jumped in and sped off.

"Come on. Jason's right. No use in everyone heading out when we have no clue who did this. Let's go inside and take another look at the board." Amy tugged on Dennis's shirtsleeve. "Jason is searching, and Kyle will take care of the evidence."

Dennis knew Amy and Jason were right. But he itched to go search for Charlotte. He trudged up the three steps and into his house, followed by Keith and Amy.

Why had he blown up at her? It was completely out of character for him. His own pain had taken hold and caused him to act like a jerk, that's why.

He glanced at the coat hooks by the front door. Her jacket remained where she'd hung it. And now she was outside in the cold. If they didn't find her before nightfall, the temperatures would drop again, and without her coat, she'd freeze to death. Assuming her attacker didn't finish the job first.

"Dennis." Amy's soft voice almost undid him. "Work with us."

He pulled up a chair and stared at the board. The whole thing looked like a blurry mess. He'd gone over the names and connections so many times throughout the night that his brain hurt. But for Charlotte, he'd do it again and again until they found a lead.

They dove into the list of names for yet another time, praying something clicked.

"Charlotte knew the nurse. She said it was the same woman who helped her when she had her baby. The nurse would make the most sense, but she's dead. The attorney, Kent, and the social worker, Erin, had an argument the other day at Sadie's Place." Dennis replayed the event in his mind. The argument behind closed doors had been muffled, but he searched his memory for words or phrases that might help. He came up with nothing.

Amy toggled her pen back and forth between her fingers and studied the pages in front of her. "Troy Kent has an alibi for several of the dates. Unless he hired someone, which *is* possible, he's not the person who killed Stella and the nurse. Donna, Troy's wife, and his admin, Penny, could falsify records, so I suppose they could be involved."

Keith scratched the stubble on his jaw. "Maybe. But they had to have had an inside person. It takes some major strength to strangle someone and move a body, and Mel said that the person who strangled the nurse did it with their bare hands. I'm not sure either of those women are capable."

"Are you saying a woman can't strangle someone?" Amy's eyebrow rose.

Keith shook his head. "Not at all, but these two are on the smaller side, and I don't think either one of them has seen the inside of a real gym."

"From what I understand, the girls said Erin overheard them discussing changing their minds. People saw her holding the baby, and she's still missing. Plus, it was her car at the accident scene where we found the nurse. At this point, focusing on the social worker is our best option." Amy said.

Dennis didn't want to agree, but it made the

most sense. "If it's Erin, it will break Charlotte's heart." Assuming she's still alive.

Keith gave him a knowing look, then grabbed a laptop. "I'll start a deep dive into Erin Rivers."

Dennis's phone buzzed. His pulse raced, hoping to hear Charlotte's voice on the other end. He yanked it from his pocket and almost accidentally threw it across the room. He jabbed the answer button. "Monroe."

"Boss, it's Doug. I found Ms. Rivers."

"Hold on. I'm putting you on speaker." The door clicked closed, and Kyle entered with Theo. The dog's nails clicked on the floor as he paced around the room. "Go ahead. We're all here."

"Hospital security found Ms. Rivers's body behind a dumpster at the back of the hospital. Dr. Vogel took her body to the morgue. I told him we need the information fast and why. Believe it or not, he's getting right on it."

Keith released a long breath. "Good. Maybe he'll find evidence that will help."

"What about Ginny's baby?" Amy asked.

"No sign of the infant."

Wonderful. They'd found Erin, but not the missing baby. "So Ms. Rivers is not our suspect." Dennis didn't know whether to feel relieved that it wasn't Charlotte's friend and coworker or disappointed because they had to try again for a lead on the person who'd abducted Charlotte and had wreaked havoc on pregnant teens. "Thanks for letting us know. Stay with the body. Let me know when Vogel finishes the preliminary autopsy."

"Will do." Doug disconnected, leaving Dennis numb from the information.

Kyle tapped the back of a chair. "Jason found tire tracks on the county road several miles from your house and is following them. It's not much, but it's worth a shot."

"I'll take it." Dennis retrieved his coat and Theo's leash, relieved to get out there and search. Sitting around the house was driving him crazy. "Keith, Amy, stay here and see what else you can dig up. Kyle, you're with Theo and me. If anyone can find Charlotte, it's her dog."

Kyle grabbed extra layers and pointed to Theo. "You think he can find her?"

Did he? "I sure hope so." He patted Theo's head. "You can do it, right, boy?"

The dog looked at him as if to say *hurry up*.

Kyle jangled his keys. "I'm driving."

Good. Dennis didn't want to admit to his deputy that his nerves were a jumbled mess. He let Theo in the back and jumped in the passenger seat.

Kyle cranked the engine and pulled from the driveway. He turned right and drove at a snail's pace, giving them the opportunity to scan the woods on either side of the road for anything out of the ordinary.

Snowflakes drifted in the air, tapping the windshield. Dennis closed his eyes at the unfairness of the situation, then glanced at the dashboard. The temperature read twenty-six degrees. That, mixed with the snow, worried him.

Was Charlotte somewhere inside and warm? Or was hypothermia her worst enemy right now?

His gaze painstakingly ran along the side of the road. The untouched snowdrifts that spanned over the ditch and curved into the tree line diminished his hopes. No tire tracks or footprints. He held on to the fact that Jason preceded them, still following the tracks of a truck that they assumed the attacker had parked out of sight of Dennis's house and used to abscond with Charlotte.

God, I really need Your help right now. Could You give us a hint? Anything?

"We'll find her." Kyle's attempt to comfort helped, but Dennis knew the reality.

Between the weather and the fact that someone had tried to eliminate Charlotte on multiple occasions didn't give him a lot of hope.

"Right." Dennis drummed the armrest. "But will it be before or after that maniac kills her?"

TWELVE

Charlotte struggled against the weight holding her eyelids closed. Her hands and feet were numb, and shivers wracked her body. The cold wrapped around her like tentacles. Where was she? And why hadn't Theo snuggled in to keep her warm?

"Miss B, please wake up." A whispered voice tugged at her.

She forced her eyes open and blinked several times. Her surroundings finally came into focus. A rustic cabin with a small light off to the side. The missing teen sat beside her. Or was her sight playing tricks on her? "Hannah?"

"Yeah, it's me." The girl tucked a blanket around Charlotte.

"Where are we?"

"I'm not sure. Out in the middle of nowhere."

Charlotte rubbed her forehead. "How long was I out?"

"The guy dumped you here a few minutes ago

and left. So probably not long." Hannah's hand spanned her belly, and she gritted her teeth.

"Hannah?"

The girl closed her eyes, took a deep breath and opened them.

Charlotte shimmied up to a seated position and regretted the movement, but she pushed the dizziness aside and studied Hannah. "You're in labor, aren't you?"

Tears trickled down the teen's cheeks. "Yes." She lowered her voice to a whisper. "But don't say anything. He only wants my baby."

Charlotte understood what Hannah hadn't said.

The teen was dead as soon as she delivered the baby, and she knew it. To be a pregnant teen giving birth in a rustic cabin and knowing her life was over right after—Charlotte admired Hannah's strength.

But why had the man kidnapped Charlotte and not killed her? He'd tried to dispose of her since she'd found Stella. Her shoulders drooped at the realization. He'd killed the nurse for whatever reason, and now he had no one to deliver the baby. He'd delegated her for that duty. That's why she wasn't dead. She massaged her temples in an attempt to relieve the pounding in her head from the drugs the man had used on her.

"What are we going to do?" Hannah repositioned the pillows behind her back.

"Hang in there. Give me a minute, okay." Or thirty. The cushion under her was comfortable enough, but the cold air nipped at her arms. Her teeth chattered, and she wished for a sweater as she took inventory of the room through the minimal light. Dirty but not disgusting. A small bathroom off to one side sported a light. An old-fashioned space heater in the corner hummed, working hard to chase away the chill in the tiny room. She squinted. "Is that a cooler over there?"

The teen added another blanket around Charlotte and tugged it tight. "The guy left me food and water. Plus, a stack of blankets. The heater's made it bearable, but…" Hannah's shoulder lifted.

Mighty thoughtful of him. "How long has he held you here?"

"I'm not sure. He threw me in here and locked the door right before the snowstorm." The girl tightened the blanket around her. "The wind was horrible. I thought the whole place would come down on me. And if the electricity had gone out, I'd have frozen to death." Hannah's words came out in a sob.

Charlotte remembered that night. Less than seventy-two hours ago, she and Theo had begun the search for Hannah. She and Dennis had taken refuge in the makeshift cave when the snowstorm hit. He'd protected her and almost lost his life.

Her mind drifted to Dennis's daughter and how

he'd sacrificed his time for Charlotte. And what had she done? Taken his harsh words and allowed them to cut deep. The man had reasons on top of his reasons for questioning her. If only she'd kept her cool and let him calm down. She could have explained and eased his worry. But no, she'd let her anger take control, and look where it had gotten her.

Charlotte turned her attention back to Hannah. "You survived."

"But for how long?"

Charlotte had no words, so she said nothing.

The girl's breathing quickened.

She turned to the teen. "Another contraction?"

Hannah nodded.

"You've got this. Breathe through it." She clasped the girl's hand and held onto it until the contraction passed. She knew the teen had hours before the baby came, but what about the man who'd abducted them? "Better?"

"Thank you. I was so afraid I'd be alone."

Charlotte understood that feeling and never wanted her girls to go through this by themselves. While they had time, she needed answers. "Did you recognize the man who took you?"

The teen shook her head. "I don't think I've ever met him."

Maybe if she had a description, she'd be able to identify him. "Do you remember what he looked like?"

Mouth twisted to the side, Hannah scrunched her forehead. "Tall and a little pudgy. He had brown hair and a beard. He was old, like in his forties."

The age comment made Charlotte want to laugh. Well, it *was* through the eyes of a teenager. Disappointed that the details Hannah provided were vague, she dug for more. "Anything specific like a scar or mole maybe?"

Hannah shifted on the cushion, obviously trying to find a more comfortable position. "Not that I can think of." She froze. "Wait. He had a tattoo. I couldn't see the whole thing, but it looked like a tail on his neck."

Charlotte gasped. It couldn't be. *Oh, please, God. No.* "A tiger tail?"

"Yes. Why? Do you know who it is?"

Unfortunately, she did, and it hurt her heart to even say his name aloud. "Jerry Parker."

Hannah tilted her head. "Who's that?"

"The man that runs the homeless shelter in the next town over. He helped me when I needed a place to stay. If it weren't for him, I don't know what I would've done." She scrubbed a hand over her face. "He helped Ginny and Stella too. Brought them to Sadie's Place."

"Then why is he doing this?"

Charlotte shook her head. How had she so misjudged the man? Why hadn't she seen his motives?

"To have access to babies." Her words came out as a whisper. The man she'd thanked more times than she could count had fooled her since day one. The realization made her want to throw up.

"What's he going to do with my baby?" Tears dripped off Hannah's chin.

Charlotte bit her lip. Did she dare tell the girl the truth? Or at least what she suspected?

"Miss B. You've always given it to me straight. Don't start lying to me now."

She had vowed to each girl that she'd be honest with them. About their situation. About life in general. Their current circumstances didn't change that promise.

"I think he's selling the babies." The pieces fell into place. "You, Ginny and Stella changed your minds about the adoptions. I'm guessing he couldn't let that happen."

The door opened, and freezing air blew in. "You're right. I couldn't." Jerry Parker stood in front of them, a cocky smile on his face. "Good to see you, Charlotte."

"I wish I could say the same."

"Tsk-tsk. Why the hostility?" He laughed and turned his attention to Hannah. "And how's our little momma doing?"

Hannah cowered behind Charlotte.

"No need to be afraid, darlin'. I just want to make sure that baby is healthy."

Charlotte grabbed Hannah's hand and rubbed up and down her arm, hoping to comfort the young girl. Hannah's grip grew tighter. No, not now. Jerry couldn't know the baby was coming soon.

The girl's contractions had sped up at an alarming rate. What Charlotte thought would be measured in hours now bordered on minutes. An extensive first-aid course, along with her own experience, had her estimating the baby's arrival in an hour or so.

Her brain scrambled for a distraction to draw Jerry's attention from the teen. "When did you turn into a criminal?"

He closed the door and folded his arms across his chest. "Really, Charlotte? That doesn't matter."

"It does to me." And it did because she'd changed her mind, just like these girls. Would she have ended up like Hannah, or dead like Stella if her baby hadn't died? But none of it mattered. She moved to hide Hannah's face.

Jerry studied her and shrugged. "If you must know, you were one of mine. The day you walked into the homeless shelter was the day fortune smiled down on me. I had a buyer and no girl. Then you came along and solved my problem."

"But my baby died."

A grin formed on his lips. "It all worked out."

Confusion ran through her mind. How had it worked out? The baby he wanted—her baby—

had died. Hadn't she? Was it possible? She shook off the thought, refusing to go there. "Did you find another girl last minute or something?"

"Or something." The sneer on his face sent shivers racing down her spine. The man she'd thought saved her life was pure evil. "Now, if you'll excuse me. There's a homeless girl waiting for my help." His gaze drilled into Hannah. "That baby better get here soon, or I'll have to take matters into my own hands." With that, Jerry spun and slammed the door shut behind him and slid what sounded like a brace into place.

Charlotte's thoughts went to Stella. She put her arm around Hannah and pulled her close. She refused to let Jerry take the life of another one of her girls.

She needed a plan, but with Hannah in labor, it limited her options. She prayed Dennis hadn't given up on her, and he was out there searching.

Because she had a very bad feeling about what would happen the next time Jerry Parker came back to the cabin.

The cold air snuck under Dennis's coat collar. He traipsed through the snow to where Jason crouched, studying tire tracks. "What do you have?"

"Not much." Jason examined the area around them.

"That's not what I want to hear."

Jason lifted his gaze to meet Dennis's. "Yeah, I get that. But it's the truth."

"You said not much. That means you have *something*. Go ahead."

"Based on the size of the tire impressions, whoever it was owns a truck or SUV."

"Well, that narrows it down." Dennis couldn't help the sarcasm dripping from his words.

Kyle walked up behind him. "I'd say calm down, but I know what it's like to lose the woman you love."

"I don't—"

His deputy waved a hand at him. "Tell yourself whatever makes you feel better, but it's written all over your actions."

"He's right." Jason stood. "I've never seen you lose your cool. You're the most levelheaded and chill person I know."

"You seem to have forgotten the day Amelia landed on my doorstep."

Jason chuckled. "I'll give you that one. You were a hot mess. But you never snapped at anyone."

He opened his mouth to disagree, but that day played in his mind. Confusion, worry and fear had topped his emotions. Then love had covered them all. Yes, anger had crept in and still did from time to time when he thought about what Amelia's mother had done, but he'd never let more than frustration take hold.

Out of everything that had happened in his life, the one time he'd lashed out was at a woman he had no relationship with other than a new friendship. He closed his eyes and inhaled. Okay, so the guys might be on to something. He hadn't intended to fall in love with Charlotte. It had just slowly happened over the past couple of days. In fact, he hadn't even realized it until now. He'd cared for her, yes. But love?

Dennis sighed. "Point taken. Now, can y'all quit analyzing my love life, or lack thereof, and help me figure out where Charlotte is?"

"The tire tracks curved back onto the road, but—" Jason pointed in the distance "—there are footprints over there. And whoever left them knows how to hide his tracks beyond the tree line."

"Great." Dennis stared off into the woods, his mind racing. The woman he'd fallen in love with was in the hands of a madman. What if he lost her before he had the chance to apologize and tell her how he felt?

"Yo, boss." Kyle smacked him on the back.

"Sorry. Lost in thought."

"We could tell." Kyle hitched a thumb over his shoulder. "What do you say we try that dog of hers, and see if he can find her?"

The trio trudged over to the vehicles and gathered their emergency backpacks and additional winter gear. But what did he have of Charlotte's for Theo to work with? "Hold up, guys." He dialed Keith's number.

"Young."

"Keith, it's Dennis. I need an article of Charlotte's clothing, or something that has her scent on it."

Keith snickered.

Dennis rolled his eyes. "You are such a ten-year-old. For her dog, you dipstick."

"I'm on it. Drop a pin on your location, and I'll be there as soon as I can."

"Thanks."

He disconnected the call and marked his location on his phone, then relayed the information to Kyle and Jason.

His deputies leaned against his SUV while he paced alongside it. The guys and their stupid observations. Now his anxiety had ramped up at the idea of losing the woman he loved. He could see the headlines now. Local sheriff falls in love. He wanted to laugh at the absurdity, but he lived in a small town, and rumors tended to spread faster than a cheetah ran.

"You need to save your energy, man."

He pivoted and glared at Kyle. "Thanks for the recommendation."

Jason elbowed Kyle. "See. Told you he's in love."

"Would you two knock it off?" The two comedians he *used* to call his friends weren't helping matters. The longer he waited, the worse his imagination got.

Fifteen minutes later, Keith parked behind his department vehicle. "I grabbed the scarf from her coat and put it in a bag. I hope that'll work."

"You and me both." Dennis took the item from his deputy and opened the back door of the SUV. Theo joined him at the edge of the seat. "What do you think, Theo? Can we work together to find Charlotte?"

Theo barked, then jumped out and sat. His brown doggy eyes stared up at Dennis as if to say *what's taking so long*?

Dennis clipped on the leash and closed the door. "Come on, boy." He and Theo joined the others.

Keith, decked out in his winter gear, gestured toward Theo. "You know how to drive that thing?"

He'd asked himself that very question not that long ago. "Not really."

"Let's hope the dog is smarter than we are." Kyle clipped the front straps of his backpack.

Jason nodded. "Amen to that, brother."

Dennis shook his head at his friends. He knew they intended the levity for him, and he appreciated the effort—and it helped at the margins. "If you're done now." He knelt beside Theo and held open the bag. "Okay, boy."

Theo tilted his head as if to ask *what do you want me to do?*

"Come on, Theo, help me out." Dennis sighed and searched his memory. He remembered the command *Find*, but what had Charlotte said to the dog for him to sniff the clothing? "*Check*?"

The dog sniffed the scarf.

Hallelujah. He'd accidentally gotten it right.

Dennis rose and unclipped the dog's leash. "*Find*."

Theo sniffed and zigzagged by the tire marks then shot off through the trees, the animal's nose and tail high in the air. "Let's go, gentlemen." Maybe he should have left the leash on, but he wasn't as skilled as Charlotte, so it was better to follow the dog's lead.

Breathing heavily, he slogged through the snow, attempting to keep up with Theo. But the dog had found the scent and bounded through the woods.

"Man, that dog can run." Kyle huffed and puffed next to Dennis.

"I sure hope we don't lose him," Jason called out.

Afraid if he halted the dog's progress, he'd lose the scent, Dennis debated stopping him so they could catch up. Yet, if they lost him… "Theo, *come*."

Keith bent over and placed his hands on his knees. "And I thought I was in shape."

"We're all upping our PT once this is over."

The men grumbled.

Theo trotted back and sat.

"Okay, boy, can you slow down so we can keep up? The snow isn't easy to run through." Great. He was trying to reason with a dog.

Theo tilted his head to one side, then the other.

Dennis checked the time, and his heart sank. Between the dropping temps and a killer on the loose, the longer Charlotte remained missing, the greater the risk he'd find her dead. The thought of losing her made his stomach twist.

Enough resting. After they found Charlotte, they could take a break. Until then, no more interrupting Theo's search for their personal comfort. "*Find.*"

Theo shot off like a torpedo, and Dennis kicked it into high gear.

Ten minutes later, an old cabin appeared in the distance. "Theo, *come.*" The dog returned, but Dennis sensed the animal wanted to keep going. "Is that where she is?"

The dog sat and yipped.

"Shh. Keep it down, boy. We don't want them to know we're here." He scratched Theo's head for a reward. Making the assumption that Charlotte was in the cabin, Dennis turned to his deputies. "Let's move in, but keep quiet until we know what we're up against."

The group hung tight against the trees, stealing their way closer to the small building. Theo seemed to understand and stuck next to Dennis's leg.

A crunching sound caught his attention. He held his fist in the air, and his men froze.

Someone paced outside the cabin for a few minutes, then went to the door, turned away and continued the line back and forth in front of the structure.

Was that Charlotte's attacker? And had the man planned to finish her off? Or was Dennis completely wrong about the location and the person?

He glanced down at Theo and whispered. "What do you think, boy?"

A low growl met his ears. Theo's opinion matched his. That was the bad guy and the right location.

He knew deep down that Charlotte was in there. But would he find her dead or alive?

THIRTEEN

Saturday 12:00 p.m.

A newborn's cry filled the small cabin, and Charlotte wept along with Hannah.

Thank You, God, for an uneventful delivery.

She wrapped the baby in a warm blanket and placed the sweet boy in the new momma's arms. "You did it, Hannah. I'm so proud of you."

Tears flowed as Hannah took in her son for the first time. "Thank you, Miss B. I don't think I could have done it without you."

"Sure you could have, but I'm glad I was here." Charlotte cleaned up and prayed Jerry didn't return until she had figured out a plan for the three of them to get away.

Hannah snuggled her baby closer and choked back a sob. "I can't let him go. I just can't."

"We'll deal with that once we get out of here and get you and your son to the hospital." Charlotte sat next to her. "Speaking of, have you decided on a name?"

The girl's gaze connected with hers. "Charlie."

Charlotte sucked in a breath. "After me?"

Hannah nodded. "Jordan has been great, and Mom and Dad finally came around, but you're the only one who's stood by me the entire time."

"Oh, honey. I'm honored." She ran a finger down the baby's soft cheek. "He's beautiful, just like his momma."

The door flew open and cold air rushed in, but the chill that came over Charlotte had nothing to do with the temperature and everything to do with the sinister look in Jerry's eyes.

"I knew you were hiding something." His dark gaze landed on the infant. "Hand it over."

"You don't even care if it's a boy or girl?" Charlotte searched the room. She had to find a way out. She refused to let Jerry take Hannah's baby without a fight. *Come on, think.*

He rolled his eyes and shook his head, as if she'd said the dumbest thing in the world. "Doesn't matter to me if the price is right."

How could anyone be so heartless? "So that's it? It's all about the money, and it doesn't matter who gets hurt in the process?" Of course, it was. But Charlotte had to keep him talking, or she and Hannah were both dead.

"Babies are worth a lot. More than drugs ever were."

Her heart sank. The man she'd trusted had hidden his criminal side from her, and she hadn't been the wiser.

"You stole Stella's baby then killed her?"

"Hardly. I don't know how to deliver a baby, and I definitely don't get my hands dirty."

So the man had partners. Her breath hitched. Carol. Of course, the nurse was in on it. But who else? The medallion. Where had she seen it before? Why couldn't she remember?

"Now quit stalling and hand over that baby."

Charlotte searched the room for a weapon and spotted the heater in the corner. That was it. The answer to her prayer. The old-fashioned device didn't have the safety features of the newer ones. The hot metal grate gave her an idea. But could she get there in time? She squeezed Hannah's hand and eased toward the only weapon in her reach. She met Hannah's wide eyes and hoped the girl didn't think that she was leaving her alone.

As if Hannah suddenly understood, she twisted the baby away from Jerry. "No. You can't have him! He's mine!" Hannah's screams mixed with the baby's cries caused a commotion.

"Don't make this harder than it is," Jerry hollered above the noise.

"What are you going to do with us?" Hannah held little Charlie tighter.

"Well now, the baby comes with me and goes to a couple who has paid quite generously for it. And as for you and Charlotte, I think I'll just leave you out here to freeze to death. Without that little heater..." He turned to point to it.

Charlotte grabbed it and swung the hot metal grate across his face. The force made her tumble to the ground.

Jerry howled, stumbled backward and hit the floor.

"Take the blanket and run, Hannah!" She hated sending the girl out into the elements, but it was either that or die at the hands of a maniac.

Hannah tucked Charlie in close and took off.

God, let Dennis find her and baby Charlie before it's too late.

Charlotte swayed to her feet and stumbled toward the door.

A hand wrapped around her ankle, and her chin hit the floor hard, sending shards of pain through her face.

"You little—"

She kicked out her other foot and connected with the side of his head. His grip loosened, and she scrambled away on all fours.

He pushed to his feet and staggered toward her. Angry red marks marred his face. "I planned to be kind and let you freeze to death, but now you're going to pay."

Charlotte knew that as long as his focus was on her, Hannah had a chance to get away. She crab-crawled backward and bumped against the wall, trapping herself between the side of the cabin and a madman. Heart thundering in her chest as he stepped closer, her gaze darted around the small area, searching for anything to defend herself with.

Cold air flowed into the room, but sweat beaded on her forehead.

God, is this it?

Jerry towered over her and grabbed a handful of her hair. "You've ruined everything. But once you're dead and I find that brat, I'll deliver her baby to the buyers and move on to another state." He slammed her face into the wall.

White lightning flashed behind her eyes, and the pain sent bile racing up her throat.

"You won't get in the way ever again."

Charlotte closed her eyes and cringed, waiting for the fatal blow.

A young girl with a baby ran from the cabin straight toward Dennis.

Still too far away to wait on her to reach him, he raced toward her. The cell phone in his pocket buzzed for the fourth time. Someone really wanted to get ahold of him, but he'd deal with it later.

He grabbed the girl and pulled her into the trees, out of sight of the man who'd entered the cabin a few minutes ago.

"No! Let us go!"

"Easy. It's Sheriff Monroe." Dennis struggled to maintain his hold.

The teen stopped fighting and lifted her face. Her pleading eyes connected with his.

"Hannah?"

The girl nodded. "She saved my life. You have to help her."

Worry weaved through him. "Is Charlotte in there?"

Hannah tucked the baby in closer to her body. "He's going to kill Miss B."

"Go with Deputy Young." Dennis handed Hannah off to Keith. "Get her out of here." Without another word, Dennis sprinted to the cabin.

An ear-piercing scream echoed through the woods.

He yanked his weapon from the holster and prayed he wasn't too late. The footfalls behind him told him his deputies had his back. No matter what happened to him, he trusted them to make sure the man behind the kidnappings didn't get away.

With Theo by his side, he slowed, told the dog to stay, then stepped into the doorway of the one-room cabin. "Police!"

Jerry Parker held Charlotte by a handful of hair. Blistered burns disfigured his face, and blood dripped from Charlotte's split lip and a cut on her temple. Her eye had all but swollen shut. The whole scene was like something out of a horror movie.

"Don't come any closer, Sheriff, or she dies." Jerry jammed the barrel of a gun into Charlotte's temple.

Dennis held his weapon on Jerry. A hundred different scenarios flooded his mind. It didn't matter that Kyle and Jason stood outside, ready to move in. One wrong move and it wouldn't matter. "Take it easy."

"Here's how it's going to be, Sheriff. You're going to let me walk out of here with her, and I might let her live."

"Like that's going to happen," Charlotte snarled.

Dennis wanted to tell her to quit egging him on, but he had to focus on Jerry and watch for an opportunity to intervene.

"You're just a money-hungry fool," Charlotte bit out.

"Shut up!" Jerry jammed the gun harder into her temple, and Charlotte cried out.

The sound churned Dennis's stomach. What was she doing?

"What? You can't handle the truth?" Her words slurred.

Jerry yanked her hair, jerking her head back. "I told you to shut up!" Reacting to Charlotte's taunts, Jerry loosened his grip on the gun.

Charlotte twisted, reached up and raked her fingernails down the burns on Jerry's face.

Dennis charged in and tackled the man to the

ground. He clamped his hand over the butt of the weapon and struggled to keep the barrel pointed in a safe direction, but Jerry was stronger than he looked, and Dennis lay on top of him at an odd angle, making it difficult to maintain the upper hand.

Thrown to the side, Charlotte had rolled away. He hoped she'd managed to get out of the line of fire but couldn't take his attention off Jerry to confirm that she had.

Theo raced in with Jason and Kyle on his heels and chomped down on Jerry's ankle and growled.

A flurry of yells bounced off the walls of the small room. Body parts flailed, fighting for control. Jerry twisted, and the gun moved toward Dennis. He watched in slow motion as the barrel came closer and closer to his head.

He had to find every last amount of strength he had before it was too late. He clamped down harder and prayed.

The gun went off, and silence zapped the room except for heavy breathing and Theo's sharp whine.

A red mist covered the floor and wall.

Dennis hurt all over, so he wasn't sure whom the blood belonged to. He took inventory of his body parts and those of the heroic dog next to him, praying the dog hadn't taken a bullet. Then his gaze landed on the man who'd betrayed Charlotte and wreaked havoc on helpless teens.

Jerry lay lifeless beneath him.

Dennis rolled off the man and lay on his back. He stared at the ceiling, his breathing heavy and labored. The ringing in his ears from the close-range shot had triggered vertigo, and his stomach turned. He couldn't move even if he wanted to without throwing up.

Kyle towered over him. "You okay there, boss man?"

The words were muffled, but he got the gist of what Kyle had asked. He swallowed hard and closed his eyes. "I think so." He heard Jason clearing Jerry's weapon and the clank of his deputy handcuffing him per department procedure, even though the man was dead.

Fur tickled his cheek. Dennis opened his eyes. A wet tongue licked his face. He had to chuckle. "Hey there, Theo. Thanks for the assist." The dog gave one more swipe of his tongue and sat. Dennis returned his gaze to his deputy. "Where's Charlotte?"

"I'm right here." Her beautiful but swollen face came into his line of sight.

He inhaled and winced. Dennis hadn't been in a street fight in a long time. And even then, it had been in the line of duty. Jerry had gotten him good.

"Where does it hurt?" she asked.

He laughed, then moaned. "Everywhere?"

With shaky fingers, she smoothed his hair from his forehead. "I can relate."

"I see that." Dennis eased to a seated position, testing his inner ear. Once he'd confirmed that his stomach wouldn't revolt, he stood and pulled her into a hug. "How are *you* doing?"

"Worried about Hannah. Jason told me you found her, and she's on her way to the hospital with Keith."

Now that time had passed, Dennis shook uncontrollably against the fading adrenaline, and the cold wasn't helping matters.

"Dennis?"

"I'm okay. Give it a few minutes, and the adrenaline shakes will stop."

"Come here. Sit down for a second." She led him to a cushion, her own trembles evident as she pulled him next to her.

"Thanks." He knew better than to fight the reaction. Waiting it out was the only option.

Ten minutes later, he rose to his feet. His energy level had dropped to subzero, and the prospect of the hike to the SUV seemed like a marathon distance, one he had no desire to make at the moment. But he had to get Charlotte to a doctor and check on Hannah. They'd gotten their man, but the missing babies required his attention.

He turned to Jason. "Even though the guy is dead, make sure this is by the book."

"Don't worry, not my first crime scene. Mel's on her way. I've got this. Kyle, get Dennis and Charlotte out of here." Jason began snapping pictures with his phone, documenting the scene.

"Come on, boss. Let's see about medical attention for the both of you." Kyle motioned toward the door.

With no argument—simply because he didn't have the energy and Charlotte needed a doctor—Dennis escorted her out of the cabin, away from the nightmare she'd endured.

No one talked as the group trudged through the woods.

What if he hadn't made it in time? An image of Charlotte's lifeless body flickered in his mind. His breath caught in his throat. In a desperate move to dislodge the vision, he grabbed Charlotte's hand. The contact kept him in the present and prevented his mind from tumbling down a dark path.

Dennis continued the trek with Charlotte by his side, dodging downed tree limbs and stepping with caution through the accumulated snow. His mind struggled to maintain a coherent thought.

Theo pressed against Charlotte like she'd vanish if he stopped touching her. Dennis understood the feeling. The whole ordeal had him questioning why he'd ever doubted her. A story he still wanted to hear because he owed it to her to listen. But now wasn't the time or place for that discussion.

A mental list formed in his head. Get Charlotte's wounds tended to. Change out of his bloodied clothes and check in with Keith. Jerry was dead, but there was more going on than one man could orchestrate.

Charlotte came to an abrupt halt. "I remember where I know that medallion from."

He stumbled at the sudden stop and pivoted to face her. "Where?"

"A man named Rick Kepler. I met him years ago. He was the janitor at the shelter."

"Good job. Now we have a name."

"You know, I think I saw him over by Troy Kent's office next to a van. But I can't be sure."

"We'll look into it." Once he had Charlotte's injuries tended to, he'd get his deputies on locating the guy.

"Where are the other babies?" Her brown eyes pleaded with him.

His heart broke that he had no answer for her. "I have no idea, but I intend to find out."

"We have to find them."

He ran a hand up and down her arm. "We will."

The only problem…they had no clue of Rick's whereabouts, and the man who knew the details was dead.

FOURTEEN

Saturday 4:00 p.m.

Charlotte lay on the hospital bed covered with several heated blankets. Would she ever warm up?

At this point, she wondered if it had more to do with stress than actual body temperature.

The hike out of the woods had taken what felt like forever. Then they'd whisked her away in the ambulance, and she hadn't seen or spoken to Dennis since.

Okay, so only two hours had passed, but still. Where was he?

The way he'd held her at the cabin and comforted her after… She'd thought maybe he wanted her in his life. Maybe not.

She sighed at the ridiculous direction her mind traveled.

The door swooshed open.

She rolled her head to the side and spotted Dennis.

"Can I come in?" He'd cleaned up and looked

good in his black tactical pants and sheriff's department T-shirt. A few bruises on his face and arms were the only evidence of the fight for his life a little while ago.

"Sure." She tugged the blanket closer to her chin. Of all the questions she wanted to ask, she'd stick with the reason they were in this mess. "How's the investigation coming along? Have you found any trace of the babies?"

"Not yet, but Keith's following a lead. He promised to keep me updated. I plan to join him now that you're safe and I look presentable."

"I really hope you find those babies." Her heart ached for Ginny. She understood all too well what it was like to have a baby taken away. Hers by death and Ginny's by Jerry. "Have you seen Hannah?"

"I just came from her room." He lowered himself into the easy chair like a man hiding pain and crossed his ankle over his knee. "She and baby Charlie are doing well. You did a great job out there."

"Thanks. But I only assisted nature."

"Well, I'm sure Hannah appreciates everything you did."

"At least she wasn't alone."

Dennis picked at the hem of his pant leg. "About that. I'm sorry I lost it when I saw the birth records."

"You had your reasons, I know that." Sure, it hurt that he'd assumed the worst, but she really did understand his point of view.

"But it wasn't fair to you. I should have trusted you and listened."

She nodded, not knowing what else to say.

He took a deep breath. "I'm listening now."

Was she brave enough to admit how she'd gotten pregnant? His opinion of her mattered, but he already thought the worst. What could she lose at this point? "No, I didn't put Kayley's father's name on the birth certificate. But like I said, I did tell him."

Dennis leaned forward and put his elbows on his knees. "Go ahead."

"I was twenty and in college. He was older and worked for my father. We met at a company party that I attended while home on break. I'd gone to the event in hopes that maybe…"

"You'd gain your father's approval?"

"Yes. You know the cliché. I was looking for love that I'd never had. I think you can guess the rest."

He gave her a solemn nod.

"I found out I was pregnant and went to the father. He laughed at me. Told me he wanted nothing to do with the baby and that I'd ruin his chance of moving up in the company if my father found out."

The muscles in Dennis's jaw twitched. "Did you tell your father?"

"Yeah. A fat lot of good that did. He yelled at me for throwing myself at one of his employees. Then he ordered me to get out and never come back." A sob clogged her throat. "Since most of my things were at the dorm, I packed what I could in my suitcase and left. I haven't seen either one of them since."

"That was five years ago?"

She tilted her head and raised her eyebrows.

He pushed air between pursed lips. "I'm sorry, Charlotte."

"It's okay."

"No, it's not. And I didn't help matters when I accused you of not telling your baby's father." He ran a hand over his face. "I really am sorry."

"It's in the past and is what it is. I only hope you don't hate me."

His eyes closed for a moment. When he opened them, her heart almost broke at the sympathy shimmering there. "Never. I had no right to compare you to Tina. You're nothing like her. I know that. But I let her actions cloud my judgment. Please, forgive me for being a jerk."

She reached for her cup and took a sip of water, giving herself a moment to collect her emotions. After placing the cup on the tray positioned over the lower part of her bed, she rested against her pillow. The opportunity to put the past aside gave her hope. "Let's put it behind us and move on."

"Sounds good. I'd like to—" His phone rang, and he glanced at the screen. "I need to take this. Monroe… Okay…" Dennis sat up straight. "When? I'm on my way to the truck." Cell phone to his ear, he stood, strode toward the door, then turned to her. "I'm sorry, but I have to go."

She waved at him like swatting a fly.

"Thanks." His attention went back to the call, and he hurried out the door. "What was that, Kyle?"

She sunk down into the blankets and wondered what Dennis had started to say.

Even if he was willing to look beyond her past, did she want more than a friendship with him? Could she handle Amelia in her life?

Who was she kidding? All her fears had diminished. She'd fallen for the handsome sheriff and loved his little girl. But did Dennis want more, or was he satisfied with friendship?

What was she thinking? She had no idea where he stood with their relationship. And here she lay, acting like a teenager with a crush. She tossed the blanket over her head and groaned.

"What do you have, Amy?" Dennis yanked the passenger door shut as Kyle cranked the engine.

"After you told me about how Charlotte

thought she saw Mr. Kepler at the lawyer's, I took another look at the photos. I found something that bothered me in the files and made a call to Mr. Kent's office."

"And?"

"Mr. Kent confirmed my hunch. The custodian for Kent and Associates is Rick Kepler. He's Jerry's partner. Rick's been altering files at the attorney's office. He writes in the names of the adoptive parents that pay him. If anyone pulls a case file, everything is in order."

"No one ever questioned the changes?"

"On occasion, but with the four partners at the firm, Rick would change the name of the attorney, and with the volume of clients they handle, no one looked any deeper. The times when the girls changed their minds, either the babies died or the girls disappeared. Those files are missing."

"We need to find Kepler."

"Already done. Deputy Lewis has eyes on him."

"Nice work, Amy. You want a job as a detective?"

She laughed. "Not a chance."

Dennis rubbed his eyes and processed the information. "Amy, do you have the adoption files for Stella and Ginny?"

"Hold on."

He heard keys clicking in the background.

"No. Those are part of the missing ones. However, if you want my opinion, he has the documents somewhere. He's a businessman after all. And it would give him leverage if anyone decided to double-cross him."

"Thanks, Amy. I owe you one."

"And I'll collect in the form of babysitting. I want a night out with my husband."

"Done." Dennis would babysit for a month if it helped find these babies and stopped it from happening again.

He placed a call to his detectives with the new information and hurried to Kepler's apartment.

Dennis prepared himself for a long evening ahead and prayed they found the evidence they needed to find the missing babies.

Six hours later, they'd found the documents hidden in Parker's townhome and had Kepler in custody. The man spilled his guts once he knew no one was left alive to bail him out.

Dennis stood next to his SUV outside Kepler's apartment, blue and red lights strobed around him and yellow crime scene tape fluttered in the breeze. They'd done it. They'd stopped the illegal adoption ring. But there were still many unanswered questions. And missing children.

Kyle strolled over and leaned against the department vehicle. "Hey, boss man."

"What did you find out?"

"Kepler filled in a few blanks."

"Oh, yeah?"

"Yup. Jerry masterminded the whole business. Rick was desperate for cash, and Jerry manipulated him into helping."

"Was Carol in on it? Or was she an innocent victim?" Dennis had a hunch he knew the answer but wanted confirmation.

"Carol was their insider at the hospitals. She worked as a per diem nurse at four different places. Not only did she help kidnap the babies, it looks as though she's the one who forged a doctor's signature on the fake death certificates, pretending to be Dr. Simmons." Kyle shook his head. "Jerry ordered Rick to kill her. Seems like he was cleaning house."

"And Erin?"

"Rick eliminated her too."

"Sounds like Jerry used everyone he ever came in contact with."

"That's an accurate statement."

Dennis stood and rubbed his eyes. "At least we have the documents. We'll be able to find the babies now."

Kyle patted his shoulder. "We've got this. Go get Amelia and go home."

FIFTEEN

Saturday 9:00 p.m.

Dennis wanted to grab his daughter and hold on tight. He couldn't imagine all the lives that Jerry and Rick, with the help of Carol, had turned upside down with their illegal adoption business.

He pulled up to the retirement home and parked his SUV. He planned to get Amelia and take her home as soon as he thanked Judith for helping out.

Since the doctor didn't want Charlotte to be alone, Jason had seen Charlotte safely to Dennis's place before he'd joined them for Kepler's arrest. Dennis hoped she was resting after her terrifying experience.

Fatigue settled into his bones from the long day. His muscles and bruises still smarted from his struggle with Jerry. He was getting old. Or at least he felt every one of his thirty-eight years. He slid from the driver's seat and exhaled.

Dennis made his way up the sidewalk to the front door. Charlotte's face occupied his mind. At the hospital, he'd almost spilled his guts about his feelings for her. But now that time had passed, he wasn't sure. Charlotte had filled the empty spot in his heart like no woman ever had, but would she love Amelia? And had he truly gotten over the fact she hid the truth from him? He understood why she initially hadn't told him about her baby and the circumstances around it, but if she did it once, would she do it again?

Before he lifted his hand to knock, the door flew open.

"What are you waiting on?" Miss Judith eyed him up and down. "You look terrible."

"Thanks a lot." He chuckled. The older woman wasn't known to hold back her opinion.

She grabbed his sleeve and tugged him inside. "Sit down before you fall down."

"Yes, ma'am."

Judith crossed her arms. "What's going on in that head of yours?"

"I'm just tired, that's all."

"Oh, horse hockey. There's more going on up here than that." She tapped his forehead.

"Maybe." Yeah, there was more. He couldn't get Charlotte out of his head.

"Does this have something to do with that

sweet lady you had with you when you dropped off Amelia?"

He sighed and dropped onto the couch. Judith had a way of putting a person on the spot. "I want the best for my little girl."

"You don't think that's Charlotte?"

"She kept her baby and her family situation a secret." His gaze met Judith's. "That's hard for me."

Judith sat next to him on the couch and patted his arm. "Honey, what that horrid ex-girlfriend did to you was awful. But not everyone is like that."

"True."

"How long have you known Charlotte?"

He chuckled. "Less than four days."

"And you expect her to tell you her life story?" Judith looked at him like he'd bumped his head.

"It'd be nice." Dennis ran a hand over his face. He realized how ridiculous he sounded.

The older woman tsked. "You are one of the most mild-mannered men I know. But when it comes to Amelia, you're a bear."

He opened his mouth to protest, but Judith cut him off.

"You have every right to be cautious. Just remember not to push a wonderful woman away because of fear."

"I'm trying to protect Amelia." Why couldn't people understand that?

"Really? Or are you protecting yourself?"

He wanted to argue, but Judith had put him in his place. She'd slapped him with the truth, and he didn't like that version of himself. Charlotte deserved better.

He leaned over and kissed Judith on the cheek. "You're a smart woman, Judith Evans."

She swatted him on the arm. "Now, don't be getting all mushy on me."

"I wouldn't dream of it." Dennis smiled for the first time in what seemed like days.

Judith rose from the couch. "Let me get that cutie-pie for you. I think you need a hot meal and twelve hours of sleep."

"I wouldn't turn down either."

The older woman gave him a knowing look then ambled from the room to get his daughter, leaving him to mull over Judith's words.

Had he really used Amelia to hide behind his own insecurities?

The fireplace crackled, warming the living room, and Theo snored on his bed next to the hearth. Charlotte tucked her legs under her. A cup of coffee cradled in her hands, she leaned against the arm of the couch and tugged down an afghan draped over the back, then snuggled in.

Hours had passed since Dennis had left her at the hospital. Not long after, Jason had driven her to Dennis's house, told her to make herself at home, then rushed out the door.

She understood Dennis had a job to do, but her mind ran wild at what he had started to say. For the first time in five years, she considered risking her heart. The willingness to face her pain head-on by befriending a five-year-old girl had surprised her. Dennis and Amelia were worth it, but how did he feel about her?

Ugh. "Well, Theo, I guess it's just you and me again."

The dog raised his head, yawned and stretched his front legs. He ambled over and joined her on the couch.

"You're a good boy, you know that?"

As if in answer, he laid his snout on her lap and huffed.

She absentmindedly ran her fingers through Theo's fur and stared at the flickering flames. Between the fire and the blanket, the chill had finally dissipated. The bruises and cuts on her face and body were another story. She ached from head to toe, but it was her jaw where she'd hit the floor that throbbed in time with her heartbeat.

Her thoughts kept circling back to Jerry's deception and the emotional and physical pain he'd cost her and others. She'd toyed with the idea that Kayley might be alive, but her heart and head refused to go there. To do so would open her up to reliving her loss all over again when they confirmed what she already knew—that Kayley had died.

She hoped Dennis and his deputies found the babies and put everyone involved behind bars.

The front door clicked open, and Amelia's voice rang throughout the room.

"Miss Charlotte, you're here!" The girl came running in and stopped when her gaze landed on Theo. "Hey, doggy. Want to come help me get ready for bed?"

Theo flopped off the couch and sat at Amelia's feet. The girl giggled and scratched his ears, then the two disappeared down the hall.

"I guess we know who's really important." Charlotte smiled and turned her attention to the little girl's father. "Wow. You look rough. I mean... You look... I'll just stop talking now."

Dennis chuckled and plopped on the other end of the couch. He leaned his head back. "It's a day I'd rather not repeat." He got quiet, and she left him alone with his thoughts. "I'm sorry about Erin."

"Thank you. Jason explained what happened." She swiped a stray tear trickling down her cheek. "She was my friend. I'm really going to miss her. I'm just glad she wasn't involved."

He rolled his head to face her. "I'd change the outcome if I could."

"I know." She twisted the blanket and licked the cut on her lower lip. "What happened after you left the hospital?"

"We caught Jerry's partner and found enough evidence to put him away for a long time."

"Who was it?"

"You gave us the lead with the medallion. It was Rick Kepler. Jerry manipulated him from the beginning. The two set up the operation in one location for a while, then moved to a different town and different attorney's office before anyone got suspicious."

"I can't believe I trusted that man."

"He helped you when you needed it most."

"It *was* a low point in my life. But I still feel like a fool."

He reached over and clasped her hand. "Don't do that. You're an amazing woman."

"I'm not sure I agree, but I'll take the compliment."

Amelia skipped into the room and patted her dad on the cheek. "You look hungry. I'm going to fix you dinner before I go to bed." She rushed to the kitchen, Theo on her heels.

"Amelia—"

Charlotte squeezed his hand. "Don't."

"I don't want her to think she has to take care of me. She needs to be a kid."

"Dennis." Charlotte shifted and sat cross-legged. "You are a great father, and she's a well-adjusted little girl. I don't think she feels obligated to take care of you. I think she wants to."

He scratched the stubble on his jaw. "I suppose."

"She sees the compassion for others in you. You're a great role model."

"Thank you for that. And again, I'm sorry for overreacting and not listening."

"We both have had less than stellar moments since we met."

"Probably so." He sat up, placed her mug on the table and collected both of her hands in his. "I know we haven't exactly had time to get to know each other, and I'd like to remedy that."

Charlotte's heart rate kicked up a notch. "What did you have in mind?"

"First, I have a question for you."

"Go ahead."

"I'm too old to not be upfront and honest and waste our time on something that can never happen."

She appreciated his frankness and understood not wanting to start something that didn't have a future from the get go. But the way he said it sent uncertainty zipping through her. "I'm listening."

"I want a family, Charlotte. Your past holds a pain that I can never fully comprehend. If you're not open to having more children after your experience, I understand. I don't want either of us to have false hope. Plus, I have Amelia to think about."

Could she open herself up to having more children? Losing Kayley had sent her into a dark abyss she never wanted to return to. But now, after getting to know Dennis and Amelia, the idea didn't seem impossible. The concept still scared her, but the all-consuming pain had vanished.

She placed her finger over his lips and smiled. "I'll forever ache over the loss of Kayley, but I'd like to give us a try. I've healed more over the past couple of days just being with you and your daughter than I have in five years. You want children. I know that and can go into a relationship with my eyes open."

A stunned expression crossed his face, and his jaw dropped. "Really?"

Had he expected her to say no? She nodded.

"All right. Okay then." He cleared his throat and took a deep breath.

She wanted to laugh at the man's nervousness.

"Charlotte, would you like to go out on a date with me?" He shook his head and laughed. "I sound like a dorky teenager."

Hand on his cheek, she smiled. "No, you don't. And Dennis, I'd love to go out with you."

A grin grew on his handsome face. He held the back of her head, gently eased her close and touched his lips to hers.

The warmth and tenderness of his kiss eased her nerves and started mending the broken pieces of her heart.

EPILOGUE

Two months later

Happy screams filled the backyard.

Dennis peeked out the window and caught Amelia and his new foster daughter, Katie, chasing the new puppy. Man, he was a sucker for those girls. He still wondered how Amelia had talked him into a four-month-old golden retriever. The furball had more energy than the girls put together.

The puppy Amelia had named Gizmo still hadn't mastered the concept that outside was the place to do his business. He tried, but accidents happened. Dennis's little family had committed to working on the issue together.

Gizmo didn't suffer from a lack of love, and the girls had flourished under the dog's affection as well.

Charlotte and Theo had left on a search and rescue call over a week ago and didn't know about the puppy or Katie yet.

He'd wanted to discuss both with her, but the snippets of time between his work and her breaks during the search never lent themselves to a good time for that talk or anything more than the little things. He missed Charlotte something horrible and anxiously waited for her to return.

For the last two months, he and Charlotte had dated as often as their schedules permitted. Many times, Amelia had joined them for a trip to the park or hiking on the Myers Lake trail. Pain no longer lingered in Charlotte's eyes when she spent time with Amelia, and the two had forged a special friendship. Something Dennis thanked God for every day.

The front door creaked open. "Knock, knock." Charlotte's voice drifted through the house.

"Come on in." Dennis shoved his hands in his pockets, suddenly nervous about the upcoming conversation.

He made his way to the entry, took Charlotte in his arms and lowered his mouth to hers, enjoying the connection. She threw her arms around his neck and deepened the kiss.

After lingering a little longer than normal, he eased back and rested his forehead against hers. He wrapped his arms around her waist. "I missed you."

"Same." She smiled.

Paws propped against his leg, and a wet tongue swiped his arm.

"Well, hello there, Theo." He scratched the dog's head. "I missed you too, buddy."

The dog barked then bounded into the house and headed straight to the back door.

Charlotte chuckled. "Guess he's ready to play."

"Hang on a second. I'll let him out. Wait here." Before she responded, Dennis let Theo outside.

Giggles and yips filtered from the backyard into the house.

"Sounds like a party out there." Charlotte took off her windbreaker and hung it on the coat hook by the door.

He hurried back. When she finished her task, he grabbed her hand and tugged her to the couch. "Have a seat. I have something I need to tell you."

She tilted her head and studied him before lowering onto the cushions. "What's going on?"

"I did a couple of things." He ran his hand through his hair. Man, this was harder than he'd expected. "I wanted to talk to you first, but everything just kind of happened."

Charlotte's brows rose to her hairline. "Well, I'm here now."

"Yeah, you are." He grinned like a fool and snuck another kiss.

She playfully slugged him. "Will you get on with it?"

"So there might be this little furball out in the backyard that insisted I bring him home."

Her laughter filled the room. "You got a puppy?"

"Maybe." He shrugged. "Okay, yes. Amelia begged, and I couldn't say no."

She struggled to keep a straight face. "You do realize at some point you have to quit giving in."

"I'll stop, I promise, but after watching her with Theo… She needed him." His daughter had blossomed into a child during the last week, and the pup had a lot to do with it.

Charlotte rolled her eyes and shook her head. "What kind is he, and what's his name?"

"He's a golden retriever."

"Oh, boy. Do you know what you got yourself into?"

Yeah, he'd figured that out pretty quickly. "He might have a lot of energy, but he… I don't know…senses when she needs him."

"Goldens are fantastic dogs, but they also have quite the personality."

"I'm discovering that. And those eyes." He shook his head.

"So what's his name?"

"Gizmo." He waited for her to laugh or tell him he was nuts.

"Original."

"Don't look at me. Amelia's the one who named him."

"And how does *Dad* feel about the puppy?" Mischief shimmered in her eyes.

The little guy had slept on Dennis's bed every night. And except for the landmines in the house, Gizmo had filled a void in his life too. Dennis hadn't realized he needed the dog as much as his daughter. "Dad's happy about it."

"That's good."

"You'll help train him?"

"Of course." She pinched her lips together, and her shoulders shook.

He narrowed his gaze. "What's so funny?"

"You do know that goldens don't mature until they reach the age of three, right?"

He sat and stared at her.

"The look on your face…" Charlotte let out a full-on belly laugh.

"Please tell me you're kidding."

"Nope. But don't worry. He won't act like a puppy that whole time. Just full of energy."

Phew. "That's a relief."

"Seriously, though. A golden is a great choice."

"He seems perfect for Amelia." He glanced at the door to the backyard and swallowed hard. "There's one more thing I need to tell you. I… um… I decided to become a foster parent."

Charlotte sat up straight. "You did?"

He nodded. "It came up unexpectedly. You see, there was this little girl Amelia's age. Her parents were killed in a car accident a year ago. Social services searched for any living relatives and came up empty."

"So you decided to step in." Her voice softened.

"More or less." How did he explain?

"Are you going to adopt her?"

He took her hands in his. "You see, that's where things get a little tricky."

"They won't turn you down because you're a single dad."

He laced his fingers with hers. "I'm hoping I won't be single much longer."

"Is that so? Are you planning to marry someone I know?" Charlotte smirked.

"I'm thinking about it." He stole a quick kiss. "But I want to make sure she's ready so that I don't scare her off."

"Good plan." She leaned in and whispered. "She doesn't scare easily."

"Trust me, I know that firsthand." Remembering how close he'd come to losing her, he squeezed her fingers. "So anyway, I brought the little girl home soon after you left on your search and rescue. She's absolutely adorable, and she and Amelia get along great."

"Sounds like you made a good choice."

"I sure hope so." He released a pent-up breath. It was now or never. "Her name is Katie, and she's five years old."

Charlotte listened, her entire focus on him.

His pulse drummed against his skin. "What I didn't say before is that I found a relative but haven't told the person yet."

"Why on earth not?"

Here went nothing. "Katie is short for Kathryn, but her original name was Kayley."

Eyes wide, Charlotte tightened her grip on his hand. "Kayley?" she whispered.

Dennis nodded. "I found your daughter."

She shook her head. "No. That's not possible."

Her pallor worried him, but he sat there quietly and let her process the information.

Charlotte stared at him. "How?"

"While we finished collecting evidence and concluded the investigation into Jerry, something kept nagging at me. I dug a little deeper, and I found the documents for the couple who adopted Katie." He used air quotes as he said the word *adopted*. "I wasn't sure what I was going to do when I located her. You see, some of the parents we discovered knew nothing about the illegal adoptions. They only wanted a child and thought the money they paid went to care for the mothers, and they were innocently caught up in the crime. And if that was the case for Kayley, I didn't want to tear her away from the only family she knew. Especially if they truly loved her.

"It took a while to track down her location. But when I found her, I discovered her parents had died in an accident, and she was in the foster care program. That made the decision easier."

"Why didn't you tell me?" Tears pooled in her eyes.

"I didn't want to get your hopes up until I knew for sure. Then you left on the search and rescue." He lifted his shoulder.

Charlotte's gaze drifted toward the door to the backyard. "Kayley's alive?"

"She is."

"Does she know?"

"Not yet. I thought it'd be better to wait until you could tell her."

A lone tear slid down Charlotte's cheek, then another and another until they flowed unchecked.

"Aw, honey. Come here." He wrapped her in his arms and tugged her to him.

After several minutes, Charlotte eased back and wiped her eyes with the heel of her hands. "I don't know how to thank you."

He rested his forehead on hers. "Would you like to meet her?"

She nodded. "Please."

Hand in hand, they joined the dogs and the girls in the backyard. He felt the tremble running through her as he wrapped his arm around her waist.

The second Charlotte laid eyes on Katie, she gasped. "Oh, my, she's beautiful."

"Just like her momma."

Charlotte rose on her tiptoes and kissed his cheek. "I don't know how to thank you."

The joy on her face almost had him dropping to one knee. But he'd save that for another day. Soon. Today was for joy and celebrating a stolen little girl returned to her mother.

"Hey, Amelia, Katie. Come here."

"Coming, Daddy," Amelia hollered back. The girls skipped over with an overenthusiastic Gizmo on their heels.

He smiled at Charlotte. "Are you ready for this?"

Her eyes glistened in the sun. "More than."

His life had taken a huge hit by Tina's actions, but Charlotte and the two girls running toward him had healed the old wounds. He and Charlotte had missed out on so much with their daughters, but he intended to remedy that if she said yes to marriage and more children.

But until then, he'd enjoy the time with Charlotte and his new little family.

Dennis smiled and watched in awe as mother and daughter greeted each other for the first time.

* * * * *

*If you enjoyed this romantic suspense story
by Sami A. Abrams,
pick up these previous titles in her
Deputies of Anderson County miniseries:*

Buried Cold Case Secrets
Twin Murder Mix-up

Available now from Love Inspired Suspense!

Dear Reader,

Thank you for reading Dennis and Charlotte's story. And we can't forget about sweet Theo. What a smart pup.

When I started this series, I knew the sheriff had to have his own story. He's such an easygoing, compassionate guy that I had to see how he'd respond to having his life turned upside down. Charlotte was the perfect person to send him in a tailspin.

I had so much fun adding Theo the air-scent dog. His character is based on a real air-scent dog that I've had the pleasure of enjoying a few lazy days with. Then there's Amelia, the super smart and almost adultlike kindergartener. I had to smile when someone commented that she acted more like a twelve-year-old. You see, I teach kindergarten, and the little girl took form when I mixed three of my students together to make Amelia. So maybe she's not your average five-year-old, but young ones like her do exist out in the world.

I'd like to send a special shout out to my agent, Tamela Hancock Murray, and to my editor, Shana Asaro. You two are the best! I absolutely love working with you.

I hope you enjoyed reading Dennis and Charlotte's story as much as I did writing it. I'd love to hear from you. You can contact me through my website at samiaabrams.com where you can also sign up for my newsletter to receive exclusive subscriber giveaways.

Hugs,
Sami A. Abrams

Get 4 FREE REWARDS!

We'll send you 2 FREE Books plus 2 FREE Mystery Gifts.

FREE Value Over **$20**

Both the **Love Inspired**® and **Love Inspired**® **Suspense** series feature compelling novels filled with inspirational romance, faith, forgiveness and hope.

YES! Please send me 2 FREE novels from the Love Inspired or Love Inspired Suspense series and my 2 FREE gifts (gifts are worth about $10 retail). After receiving them, if I don't wish to receive any more books, I can return the shipping statement marked "cancel." If I don't cancel, I will receive 6 brand-new Love Inspired Larger-Print books or Love Inspired Suspense Larger-Print books every month and be billed just $6.49 each in the U.S. or $6.74 each in Canada. That is a savings of at least 16% off the cover price. It's quite a bargain! Shipping and handling is just 50¢ per book in the U.S. and $1.25 per book in Canada.* I understand that accepting the 2 free books and gifts places me under no obligation to buy anything. I can always return a shipment and cancel at any time by calling the number below. The free books and gifts are mine to keep no matter what I decide.

Choose one: ☐ **Love Inspired**
Larger-Print
(122/322 IDN GRHK)

☐ **Love Inspired Suspense**
Larger-Print
(107/307 IDN GRHK)

Name (please print)

Address   Apt. #

City   State/Province   Zip/Postal Code

Email: Please check this box ☐ if you would like to receive newsletters and promotional emails from Harlequin Enterprises ULC and its affiliates. You can unsubscribe anytime.

Mail to the **Harlequin Reader Service:**
IN U.S.A.: P.O. Box 1341, Buffalo, NY 14240-8531
IN CANADA: P.O. Box 603, Fort Erie, Ontario L2A 5X3

Want to try 2 free books from another series? Call 1-800-873-8635 or visit www.ReaderService.com.

Get 4 FREE REWARDS!

We'll send you 2 FREE Books plus 2 FREE Mystery Gifts.

FREE
Value Over
$20

Both the **Harlequin® Special Edition** and **Harlequin® Heartwarming™** series feature compelling novels filled with stories of love and strength where the bonds of friendship, family and community unite.